The Captain's

by

Audrey Harr

Published by Audrey Harrison

*

This book was proof read by Joan Kelley. Read more about Joan at the end of this story, but if you need her, you may reach her at oh1kelley@gmail.com.

## Dedication

This book is dedicated to Julie and David Oliver and Queenie the Guide Dog.

I met Julie and David through my work with the charity Guide Dogs a few years ago. Julie is blind and deaf and is completely inspirational—and I don't use that word lightly. She is a lovely lady who helped explain to the volunteers I was training just what it's like to be blind on a practical level. Those sessions contained a lot of laughter, and every volunteer left with the confidence to approach someone who may need help. That Julie enjoys a full life the way she does just proves how wonderful and resilient she is. I don't admire many people, but she is on the top of my list.

David Oliver, Julie's husband is a true gent and a lovely man. He does so much for Guide Dogs, both alongside Julie and in his own right; the organisation would be worse off without him. He was always unfazed at whatever was asked of him and always supported me whenever he could, which I completely appreciated, and I thoroughly enjoyed working alongside him. Words seem inadequate to express how much I value him.

The dog that appears in these pages isn't based on Queenie, but I had to mention her. When working for Guide Dogs, you meet so many lovely, amazing dogs that you wouldn't think you would have favourites, but you do. She is a lovely natured dog who tries to follow Julie out of the door if she is left behind. I did enjoy my Queenie cuddles!

# Chapter 1

London – early November 1806

Alexander took a steadying breath. He might have faced the French navy without any serious thought of the danger to himself or his ship, but this was different. The noise was overwhelming, and the shadows and shapes that were constantly passing in front of him sent his mind reeling as his brain tried to make sense of the signals. He had to get away, but he was trapped. Trapped in a world of near total darkness, noise and bewilderment.

Time seemed to stretch out before him. He recognised some voices, but no one seemed to want to approach him or to offer help. For the hundredth time in recent months, he was at the mercy of others; a muscle twitched in his cheek at the frustration of it.

Eventually, he heard a familiar voice. "Critchley?" he asked, a note of desperation in his voice.

"Yes, Worthington. I'm here," his friend responded.

"Where the bloody hell have you been?" Alexander ground out. He was beyond the point of caring whether he would shock anyone who had the misfortune of hearing his base language.

"For a dance," Richard Critchley, his long-time friend replied in surprise. "I told you I had secured Miss Birkett for the first two."

Alexander glowered at Richard; he might be blind, but his face still showed clearly the feelings he was struggling with. "Get me out of here! I can't stand any more of it!"

Richard came closer to his friend and touched his arm in an act of reassurance. "We've only been here for an hour; it's your first trip out, and it's bound to feel strange. Give it time," he soothed.

Alexander gritted his teeth, the twitch in his cheek becoming more pronounced; he wanted to shout with frustration at being so dependent on others. He breathed deeply in an effort to keep himself under control; even in his present state he could not behave so abominably and do something as gauche as losing control in a room full of people. "I don't care how long we've been here; it's felt like an eternity. Get me out of this place!" The words were said quietly, but were full of anger and annoyance.

Richard was not one to give up easily, but he acknowledged that Alexander must have been feeling overwhelmed to be responding in such a way. His friend was not one for dramatic gestures; ever the cool one previously, he was now agitated. The ballroom was overcrowded and hot; it had perhaps not been the wisest place to start Alexander's return to Society. "Let me help you to the edge of the ballroom for a while. If you still feel the same after my dance with Miss Stobbard, we shall leave," Richard said. He could not leave while he had promised to dance with Miss Stobbard. Her blonde curls and rosebud mouth could easily keep most men in a ballroom, especially Richard, who had a particular interest in her.

Alexander sighed but let himself be led to the edge of the room. He was totally reliant on Richard, and it grieved him. His shoulders sagged in defeat as the men moved through the crowd. He would never normally behave so badly, but these were no longer normal circumstances. When they came to a halt, he followed Richard's lead as his friend guided him to a bench, and Alexander sat down.

"I shall leave you here and see you in half an hour. Then we can call the carriage if you wish," Richard said cheerfully before leaving his friend once more.

Alexander compressed his lips to try to prevent saying something he would regret later. He tried to school his features into what he hoped was a less forbidding expression. The next half hour was not going to pass quickly.

He had thought he was alone until he heard a gentle sigh at his left. "Hello?" he asked quietly. He did not want to make a fool of himself if he had misheard and there was no one close. With so much noise going on around him, what little perception he had of his surroundings had completely disappeared.

"Hello," came the equally quiet reply.

Alexander had no idea who he sat next to. He should wait to be formally introduced, but he decided that he would flout convention. Apart from Richard, this was the first person who had spoken to him since his entrance at the ball, and he did not wish to let the opportunity pass. He had never expected a ballroom to feel so lonely.

"Your sigh would suggest that you're as delighted to be here as I," he responded, hoping the person he was speaking to was no relation to the people holding the event. Such an insult would not be looked upon kindly.

"Oh, I don't mind being at a ball," came the clear, confident voice of a young lady, although she still spoke quietly. "It's sitting all night as a wallflower that I have a problem with."

"He sat me with the wallflowers?" Alexander asked in disbelief. It was not so many months ago that he had been considered the catch of the season, and now Richard had tucked him out of the way with the unmarriageables. He would express his views on *that* insult when Richard returned.

"Yes, but as you aren't dancing, I suppose technically you could be considered a wallflower yourself. I realise it may be a shock to the system, but it can happen to the best of us," the unknown lady responded tartly.

Alexander acknowledged to himself that he had been rude in the extreme. No young lady would want the fact that she was on the shelf to be pointed out. His reaction had been such that it was very clear what he thought about being classed as a wallflower. The gentleman in him tried to make amends. "Forgive me; I cannot see very well. It was just a comment about where I was in the room."

Amelia looked at the man beside her. She was fully aware of who he was and also under no illusion that he would never have spoken to her in normal circumstances. He was completely out of her social sphere: a successful captain of the British Navy, who had made his fortune before joining Nelson at Trafalgar. He had managed to get his men out safely when their ship had been badly damaged, but he had been injured during the skirmish. He was a hero to his men, but he had lost his sight as a result of his injury. There had been no word of him for over a year, but he had unexpectedly appeared tonight. It did not seem to be going well, she mused. He was not surrounded by his usual group of friends: strange when the only outward appearance was a line of small scars at the side of his eyes and across his forehead. Surely, even the more fickle members of the *ton* could cope with a few small scars?

"I am aware of your injury Captain Worthington," she replied. Her tone was still cool; he had offered an insult, and she stung from it. She accepted that her evenings were mainly spent with the other wallflowers, but she did not appreciate being reminded of the fact.

"Then you have the advantage of me; I beg your pardon, but I do not recognise your voice. I'm relying on a dismal memory of voices to reacquaint myself with everyone. I wish I'd taken more notice of them in the past," Alexander responded. He always listened more these days, his hearing helping to give him vital extra clues to his surroundings. It was a frustrating task not being accustomed to recognising the voices of people he had not seen in a long time.

"We have never been formally introduced; I'm usually to be found helping polish these benches along with the other unfortunates. I find moving slightly in time to the music heightens the shine with the smallest of effort. At some balls, I can almost see my face in the wood by the end of the evening," came the tongue-in-cheek response. His words had stirred her sympathy, dissolving the annoyance she felt. After all, it was not his fault she was forced to sit out the dancing.

Alexander's mouth twitched in appreciation of her humour. "In that case I wish I'd discovered them earlier. With the size of my rear, I could have saved you many minutes of work."

Amelia laughed, "The wallflower benches have been my home for over two seasons, so we are well acquainted with each other. I can guide newcomers on the best view or the best hiding place, depending on their preference, of course," she said cheerfully.

"Two seasons?" Alexander asked in surprise. That was the sign of a young lady truly on the shelf. He wondered what her circumstances were that she was so obviously unmarriageable. She did not sound ugly, if ugly had a sound. He wondered if she had no dowry. "Do you never dance?"

"Sometimes," Amelia admitted. "But very rarely, especially during evenings like this one where the cotillion went on for a full hour and a half. That reduces the number of dances of the evening, so it prevents opportunities for those of us who sit on the side-lines."

"Ah, yes, the Bakers Wife; it can be tedious to dance," Alexander admitted.

"I would argue that it's more tedious to wait for the dance to end when one is anticipating the next dance," Amelia responded.

"I can see your point, but believe me, the wrong partner can make an hour and a half seem an endless amount of time," Alexander said with feeling.

"Yes, I suppose so," Amelia said with a mock sigh. "In that instance being on the wallflower benches wouldn't seem quite so bad. I'm accustomed to it now, and it wouldn't be unbearable except for the pitying stares one gets during the evening."

"I expect I've had my fair share this evening," Alexander said.

"Yes, but at least you can't *see* them," Amelia said with feeling.

Alexander was a little taken aback at the insensitivity of the remark. "I suppose I've never seen my blindness as an advantage, but it seems that you have just shown me one," he said, a little coldly. Normally people would stumble and stutter, rather than mention his blindness, if they spoke to him at all. He was not used to anyone referring to his disability so openly, so mockingly.

"I've upset you; I didn't think!" Amelia said, putting her hand on his arm and squeezing it gently. "I'm truly sorry. I suppose it's just that you look exactly like you did prior to the battle: all stiff lipped, glowering and reserved. I thought it hadn't affected you. I apologise; I should have been more sensitive," she babbled. She had not intended to offend him; that was the last thing she wanted to do to the great Captain Worthington. Amelia cursed herself for being her usual flippant self; she really did deserve to be with the wallflowers.

"Stiff lipped, glowering and reserved?" Alexander asked in disbelief as he almost choked on the words. He would have never considered himself vain, but he was aware of his reputation as handsome and charming—when it suited him to be of course. He could give a set-down with the best of them. Washer description how people really saw him? He was stunned at the thought. "I see now that my blindness is the least of my worries!" he said, his shock clear in the tone of his voice.

Amelia slapped her free hand over her mouth in horror. The most attractive man she had ever seen in her life, and she had just insulted him—*twice*. Thank goodness he had no idea who she was. "I'm so sorry; I didn't mean it. Appearances can be deceiving; I'm sure you are perfectly amenable." Her words came out in a strangled voice; she did not know whether to laugh or cry at her mistake.

Alexander laughed at her obvious mortification. He placed his hand over Amelia's, which still rested on his arm; in her distress, it seemed she had forgotten about it. "Don't fret! I should not take offence. I have taken umbrage at anyone who skirts around my blindness, and now I'm criticising you for treating me normally. It is I who should be apologising."

"At least you can't see my embarrassment either, so I should be relieved I suppose, but please believe me when I say that I'm truly sorry," Amelia repeated.

Alexander smiled, his first genuine smile in a long time. "And I'm glad I can't see the pitying looks that you speak of. I might have caused a fight if I had."

"Well, that would certainly have made the evening more interesting," Amelia said with a longing sigh. "Would you have needed me to direct your punches?"

"Would you have done that for me? That would have been very sporting of you. I can't imagine it would be much use shadow boxing, not if the other fighter can see. I have faith in my ability but would not like such poor odds," Alexander said good-humouredly.

"No, you would certainly need a way of being able to improve your chance of winning; it would be foolish to enter into something you are never going to win. One does like a fighting chance in all we face," Amelia mused entering into the spirit of the conversation.

"Yes, I see the error of my ways in being persuaded to come to a ballroom on my first foray into Society. Critchley can be so persuasive when he wants to," Alexander said, half to himself.

"I can understand his reasoning; you have been missing from Society for quite a while," Amelia said. The fact that he did not know who she was giving her the opportunity to be bolder than she would be normally.

"Yes, more than a year," Alexander admitted. "Although it would seem my friends have not only forgotten where I live but forgotten what I look like," he said bitterly at the fact that no one had approached him since he had entered the ballroom.

"It's a harsh way to learn who your true friends are," Amelia admitted.

"Yes, although I'm even doubting Critchley; he seems to have disappeared," Alexander muttered. His companion might be charming, but he still felt out of his depth. It was strange to feel so lost when surrounded by so many people.

"I think the fact that you haven't got golden curls and deep red lips might explain his absence," Amelia said with a chuckle.

"Ah yes, Miss Stobbard," Alexander said. "Is she a diamond?"

"Oh yes, she sparkles all over the room. Her dowry probably sparkles even more than she does, which is no easy feat, for those blonde curls are perfect," Amelia said with a laugh in her voice.

Alexander chuckled "I'm sure you're right. I'm no longer surprised that Critchley has been dazzled. He always did prefer blonde hair and, with her large dowry, I'm sure he's half-way to being smitten."

"It certainly looks that way," Amelia responded, having seen the way Mr Critchley was gazing into Miss Stobbard's eyes each time they crossed on the dance.

Amelia's amusement faded when she noticed her aunt approaching with a look of disgust on her face. She braced herself for her aunt's inevitably harsh words.

"Move child! What right have you to speak to the Captain?" Amelia's aunt berated sternly. She indicated that Amelia let her sit down, which the young woman complied with. "Now go and get me some refreshments; if you can't obtain a partner the least you can do is make yourself useful."

Alexander had felt his companion stiffen before the second woman had interrupted, and his senses went on high alert. He had felt vulnerable not knowing what to expect but had relaxed when he had heard the woman's voice. He was angry at her words to his companion; the elder ladies in Society did rule the younger ones with a rod of iron, but this unknown woman had just seemed rude with her words. His thoughts were interrupted when the woman addressed him.

"Captain Worthington, how pleased we are that you have joined us tonight. Your presence has been missed these last months," the woman sitting beside him gushed.

Alexander had not liked the way she had secured her seat, but manners forced him to respond politely if not pleasantly. "Thank you for saying so, but I'm afraid you have the advantage over me. Have we met?"

"Oh of course, how stupid of me!" she trilled. "I'm Lady Basingstoke, Sir Jeremy Basingstoke's wife. The rumours said your sight loss was total, but I didn't believe them. It's obvious the rumours were true."

"Lady Basingstoke," Alexander responded, inclining his head slightly. He was not about to go into details about his sight to satisfy the curiosity of the gossips. He did remember the woman next to him; how could he forget? She was one of the worst scheming mamas Society had seen in a long time. He remembered that she had two daughters, one of whom had been so-called compromised by an acquaintance of his. Everyone who knew the gentleman in question felt the young lady had done all the compromising—with the help of her mama of course.

The marriage had happened quickly, and no one had seen the unfortunate gentleman smile since. His wife was pretty, to be sure, but she was also demanding, a compulsive gambler and had the shrillest voice imaginable. The fortune that had been secured would certainly not last forever. Everybody pitied her husband but also thought he had been foolish in allowing himself to get caught so easily.

When the second daughter had come out, all the single men had made it their business never to be in a position where they could be accused of foul play. Three years had passed, and the daughter was still unmarried. Alexander knew all of this; Richard had updated him on all the gossip before Alexander had agreed to rejoin their social circle. He was on full alert for the younger Miss Basingstoke. He might be blind, but he was single, had a fortune, and was in a very vulnerable position.

"I hope you are enjoying the evening," Lady Basingstoke said, interrupting his thoughts.

"Not really," Alexander responded honestly. "Things have changed a little since I last attended a ball."

"Of course, you used to dance so often and with such grace. To be stuck on the outside of society for the rest of your life must be a horrid thought," Lady Basingstoke said without tact.

"I find not dwelling on it helps," Alexander responded abruptly.

"Of course, of course. I know the perfect way of taking your mind off your injury. Let me reacquaint you with my youngest daughter, Serena."

Alexander realised that Serena must have been standing nearby waiting for the introduction and immediately felt like a hunted animal. He could not show weakness before the two wolves, or they would probably just move in for the kill.

"Miss Basingstoke," He nodded in the direction he had felt rather than saw movement.

"Captain Worthington," Miss Basingstoke responded in the same shrill voice of her sister. "It's a pleasure to see you. I mean, oh dear, I should not have said that! I meant to say nothing about your eyes; of course you can't see; everyone knows that. I mean...." The girl continued to fumble and made the unintentional mistake worse by trying to correct it.

"Miss Basingstoke, unless you have been struck by blindness, which I sincerely hope not, you can see me. Do not fret over your perceived error," Alexander said a little coldly. He had not been troubled by her words; it was her attempt at trying to make amends in such a blundering way that was the problem for him. He did acknowledge that in some respects people could not win with his situation; he had been offended by the first young lady for being blasé about his affliction and now this. He sighed and wished himself a hundred miles away.

"Oh, you are too kind. I am sure you are too kind," Lady Basingstoke interjected. "Serena looks positively ready to faint with embarrassment. Poor girl, she meant no offence; I'm sure she just needs a little time to gather herself, and all will be well. Why don't you accompany her for a walk in the gardens while she recovers her balance, Captain Worthington? I'm sure the air will do you both the world of good."

"That would be very kind of you Captain Worthington. I would like that very much," Miss Basingstoke murmured.

Alexander almost laughed at the obviousness of the two women before him but managed to maintain his composure. "I'm afraid I will have to decline. I'd hate to be in the situation where Miss Basingstoke is taken ill and, because of my condition, I could not help her. We would be safer if we remained in this crowded room where there are people to come to our aid if needed," Alexander responded pleasantly. Inside he was congratulating himself for his quick thinking; he was not a successful ship's captain just from good luck alone. He had outmanoeuvred skilled sailors in his time; he was not about to fall prey to two scheming women.

Lady Basingstoke muttered something to her daughter but then turned to someone who had approached her. By her words, Alexander concluded it was his previous companion, but she said nothing and was soon sent away once again by Lady Basingstoke. He wanted to know who the young lady was but to ask would be inappropriate. She had not been introduced, which probably meant she was someone of little consequence. Alexander felt a stirring of regret at the thought; even on such short acquaintance she had been the most entertaining person he had met in many months.

Everyone he had met since his return home had either avoided mentioning his injury or had made similar blundering errors as Miss Basingstoke had done. Apart from Richard and Alexander's elder brother, the unknown lady had been the first person to face his blindness straight on and, although he reacted badly to it at first, on reflection he appreciated it. She also appeared to have a similar sense of humour as he, which he found unusual in ladies. It was a pity their paths had never crossed before the accident.

Lady Basingstoke was prevented from making any further progress with Captain Worthington due to Richard's reappearance.

"Good evening, Mr Critchley," Lady Basingstoke said with a smile at the new arrival.

"Good evening, Lady Basingstoke, Miss Basingstoke," Richard said with a bow. "I hope you are well?" Richard was fully aware of the Basingstokes and, although polite, he was under no illusion but that he would also be a target for the husband-seeking mama. He did not have the fortune that she wished for her second daughter, but he was comfortable enough to make him an attractive candidate after three seasons.

"I am very well, thank you. I was just saying to Captain Worthington what a pity it is that he is no longer able to dance; Serena so loves to dance," Lady Basingstoke said, turning her attention to the newcomer.

Alexander almost laughed out loud at her remarks. They had not mentioned a thing about dancing, but it was obvious he had escaped their attention, for now at least, while a fully able-bodied person was available. He listened, interested to see what excuse Richard would invent.

Richard smiled at the ladies, his dark eyes twinkling. "That is a real pity! My friend was a good dancer, I agree. I believe his conversation isn't too tedious for ladies, either," he said amiably. "Unfortunately, I'm going to have to spirit him away; my carriage awaits."

"Oh," Lady Basingstoke's disappointment was evident in her face and tone of voice. "That is a shame, but if your carriage awaits you there will be no opportunity of Serena dancing with you. What a pity! I shall bid you good night gentlemen. Serena, come, I see Lord Entwistle."

The two ladies left the gentlemen. Richard breathed a sigh of relief. "Come, Alex, let us make our escape before Entwistle gives them the brush-off. I don't want to be here when they start to look for another victim." He touched his friend's arm with his own, and Alexander placed his hand on it. They started the difficult task of negotiating a busy ballroom. With every apology Alexander had to give when he came into contact with someone, knocking them because they had not made enough room for the bulk of himself and Richard moving side by side, he vowed to himself he never would grace a ballroom again.

# Chapter 2

Amelia had watched her aunt with Captain Worthington with a sinking heart. She had no false hope that her brief conversation with him would lead to anything. He would not fall for her own charms, especially as he did not even know of her existence. Her discomfort was more to do with watching her aunt and cousin fawn over a man purely because they thought he was an easy target. It was behaviour she would never understand. They did not seem to realise they were avoided by single men as much as possible. It would have been laughable if had been happening to someone else; unfortunately the humour in the situation was not as evident when it involved members of her own family.

Amelia had been forced on her aunt. Her father and Sir Jeremy Basingstoke were brothers. Amelia's father had married for love not money and had led a very happy life with his wife and family. Having only one daughter and eight boys, he had appealed to his older, wealthier brother to take Amelia under his wing in order to help her secure a good match. He had waited until she was twenty, unusually late, but the loving father had been reluctant to say goodbye to his only daughter too early. Amelia's uncle was amenable to an extra person in his household; it would dilute the number of interactions he had to tolerate from his wife and girls. As it turned out, it was even better than he had hoped.

Amelia was blessed with rich chestnut hair and deep brown eyes; her manner was quietly confident and, although not stunningly pretty, she was considered to have pleasing features. Her mother and father hoped for a comfortable match for their daughter; Amelia would have been happy with such. She had no false illusions: She had no dowry to speak of and was not classically beautiful; she hoped only to attract a good man who she could love and be comfortable with. She had seen what contentment a loving marriage could bring and hoped to have the same.

Everything should have gone unassumingly to plan, except for one thing: Lady Basingstoke. She had her youngest daughter to marry off, and she was determined to marry her well. Amelia would have none of her attention until then, and even then only a little. Lady

Basingstoke disliked Amelia; she was not as pretty as her own daughters, but she had something else: poise, confidence and grace. It soon became Lady Basingstoke's aim to drag the girl down and send her back to her parents unmarried and worthless.

While Amelia stayed with them, Lady Basingstoke had no compunction in using her as an unpaid servant. She was giving the girl food and board and escorting her about town. Admittedly, she introduced her to only a few people, and she made it clear that the girl came with nothing but her connections to herself to recommend her. Needless to say on such a recommendation, Amelia had sat out more dances than she had danced. Most treated her with the same suspicion with which they treated Lady Basingstoke and her daughter, presuming that she would also be prepared to force a compromising situation in order to obtain a marriage proposal.

If Amelia had been of a different disposition she would have lost her spirit because of the way she was treated, but she was far more philosophical about the whole situation. It was beyond her control to alter it at the moment, but she hoped that by the end of the season, which would be her third, her parents would be more amenable to her returning home. She would have to accept that she would remain single and unwed. While her aunt was her promoter, there would be no marriage for her.

While out in Society she had seen men like Captain Worthington from afar. They were the top of the tree, the men most sought after. In Captain's Worthington's case, she could understand completely why he was in that position. Amelia had never been introduced to him but, during her first season, every time he had been at the same parties she had attended, she had been aware of his every move.

There was no possibility that Amelia would have got carried away and imagined a romance and proposal from such a man; she would never allow herself to indulge in such foolish thoughts. It did not mean she could not appreciate the rich black hair worn in a queue, as was the fashion of naval men, and his swarthy complexion, which faded the longer he was away from his ship. There was no harm in admiring such a fine man, which is only what all the ladies around her did, so she was no different on that score.

He was paler now, months having passed since he had been involved in that fateful battle. His blue eyes seemed to be made of the sea he was so fond of, although they no longer flitted around the ballroom as they had previously. He was of large build, almost straining out of his frock coat, which hugged him just as his naval uniform had done. His features matched his size, his long nose and full mouth, which complemented the eyes that initially drew one's attention. He was a devastatingly handsome man, who perhaps had not smiled overly much but had had the confidence of one who felt indestructible and completely in control.

That was how things had been. When he appeared at the present ball, Amelia had seen him from across the room. He had been openly stared at by many of his so- called friends, who whispered and tittered to each other. The gentleman who had accompanied him had seemed oblivious to the commotion, but sometimes, when one is wrapped up in seeking out a pretty face as Richard had been, other things are not noticed. No one had approached the pair, a far cry from previous entertainments when Captain Worthington would have been hailed from all directions. Amelia had been annoyed when he was so obviously shunned by his former friends.

To her it was just another representation of how shallow the Society was she belonged to while staying with her uncle. She would not be sorry when she could leave it behind and return to her own family. She understood why her father had wanted her to come to London; she just wished she could have had at least one of her brothers with her for company. That way she could have ridiculed what she had seen and treated the whole experience as a joke; instead she had to keep it contained within, and sometimes she became angry at what she saw—never as much as she had when Captain Worthington had been ignored though. She could have shook half the people in the room. Instead, she had sat on her hands and ground her teeth. Her inner self would have chuckled if she had not been so annoyed; with the glaring expression she no doubt wore, it was little wonder she had not received any requests to dance.

Amelia sighed, her life had been lonely since her arrival in London; she was not accepted or befriended by her cousin Serena. Serena took the lead from Lady Basingstoke, barely acknowledging Amelia unless it was to utter a demand or an instruction. Amelia thought it was a pity her cousin had chosen that path. She would have welcomed a female friend after being surrounded by so many brothers.

Her life had fallen into a regular pattern, which consisted very often of her choosing activities on which her aunt and cousin would not accompany her. Escaping her relations maintained her sanity since she was so far away from those she loved, who would have normally offered her the companionship she longed for. The only friend she had in town was the uncontrollable St Johns dog that her uncle had bought to accompany him on hunting trips; he had very quickly decided the dog was useless and had discarded him. The staff in the London house tried to look after him, but he was a large dog and without training had become unruly. Amelia's uncle insisted on keeping him only because of the amount of money he had paid for the dog; he was reluctant to acknowledge the substantial loss he would undoubtedly face if he tried to sell the animal.

Amelia liked the undisciplined beast. He was big and chunky; his size frightened many who came into contact with him, but he was actually very friendly. His name was Samson, which suited him as his coat was long, blonde and curly. It was true that he was unruly, but she had some sympathy with the animal; she felt like being unruly herself sometimes when she saw the way her extended family carried on. She tried to take Samson out every morning for a long walk. She was always awake before the rest of the family, and a long walk quietened him down eventually. There was no need to take a servant to accompany her; it was early, and the people who would comment on her lack of chaperone were still cosy in their beds. She doubted if any comment would be made even if she were seen; she was under no delusion as to her low importance. When she was with Samson, she felt completely safe; few people would approach her with her golden guardian at her side.

Samson seemed to understand that she was the outsider in the family and, although still unpredictable, he was gentler with Amelia than with any of the other members of the household. She took him into Green Park each morning, following different routes to try to keep alive his interest in his surroundings. He was always very excited when they first set out, running a long way ahead of her, but always running backwards and forwards between Amelia and the latest smell he had found.

She enjoyed the peace of the park during the early morning. Later on it would be full of fashionable people wanting to see and be seen, just as Hyde Park was, which was not so very far away, but there was hardly anyone around in the park during the morning. She was able to wander and enjoy the feel of being in the country, even if it was a false feeling. A country girl at heart, she missed the pleasures the countryside could bring.

The morning after yet another ball where she had joined the other wallflowers for the evening, she went out walking as usual. It had been a late night, but as she had sat out most of the dances, she had not been overly tired when she finally went to bed. She had risen as usual and taken her favourite route into the park.

As they wandered, Samson started to bark excitedly, and Amelia groaned to herself. He had seen someone, and she would have to move quickly, or they would be greeted by Samson jumping up to say hello in his own special way.

"Here boy!" she said, moving towards the animal. With a sidelong glance at Amelia, the dog ran off across the grassland. Amelia groaned and started to run after him; the quicker she got there, the sooner she could start apologising.

Two men were walking towards her and, with a sinking heart, she realised it was Captain Worthington and his friend, Mr Critchley. She picked up her speed; the last thing she needed to happen was for Samson to jump up at Captain Worthington. He could cause him some injury, and the man had been through enough lately; she did not wish to be the cause of any further suffering.

"Samson, come here!" Amelia gasped as she tried to close the distance between herself and the dog.

Alexander heard the sound of Samson running; although he had no idea what the sound was, he also heard Amelia's shout. He stopped when he heard Richard mutter, "What the hell?"

Richard stepped in front of Alexander, hoping to deflect the dog from its collision course with his friend. Surprisingly though, as the dog approached, it slowed down and came to a panting halt in front of them. Richard happy that his friend was not going to be bowled over, returned back to Alexander's side.

"What on earth is going on?" Alexander asked, once more frustrated at his helplessness and reliance on others.

"A beast of a dog not under control, and a waif of a girl who must own him, bringing up the rear," Richard said, his tone showing how annoyed he was.

Samson stood watching both men before seeming to turn his focus on Alexander and stood looking at him intently. The dog then moved towards Alexander. He approached slowly and circled around the back of Alexander's legs, touching him the whole time with his body, before sitting at his left side, nudging his muzzle under his hand for a stroke.

Alexander laughed at the behaviour. "He doesn't appear to be much of a beast at the moment," he said scratching the top of the dog's head, much to Samson's appreciation. The dog leaned against Alexander's legs, his tongue lolling to the side.

Amelia came to a screeching halt in front of the two gentlemen in a far less dignified way than Samson had. "I'm so sorry," she said, gasping for breath. "There isn't usually anyone around at this early hour, or I wouldn't have let him off his lead."

"I would doubt someone of your size would be able to hold him back even if he were on the lead," Richard said cuttingly. "You should have more control of him; he could cause some damage."

"I'm truly sorry. He's big and clumsy but not vicious," Amelia said with a flush at Mr Critchley's cutting tone.

Alexander recognised the voice; he was sure it was the same one he had heard a few nights ago at the ball he had attended. His pulse quickened at the thought of being able to find out who the young lady was. "He doesn't seem to be causing any problems now, so there is no harm done," he responded reassuringly. Samson seemed to understand; his tail thumped on the ground at the words. "He seems a friendly enough fellow."

"He's not usually so polite," Amelia admitted with a wry smile and a surprised look in Samson's direction. "His normal greeting is to jump up and lick whoever's face he decides looks most appealing."

"Well thank goodness I didn't look tempting," Alexander responded with feeling.

"You must be losing your touch, Alexander; you are usually considered very attractive to everyone you meet." Richard could not resist the jibe.

"Once upon a time maybe, but now they are afraid that blindness is catching," Alexander said with a touch of bitterness.

"That would make the remainder of the season interesting if it were. Balls would be far more entertaining than they are at the moment; it would be blind man's bluff meets the quadrille," Amelia said flippantly.

Alexander laughed, now absolutely convinced it was the same lady he had met at the ball. "That is twice now you have prevented me from going into a maudlin state, Miss —?"

Amelia flushed; every etiquette said she should not be talking to these two gentleman as she had not been previously introduced to them, and she certainly should not be introducing herself. It went against every rule of polite society. "I—er—," she stuttered.

Richard looked closely at the girl. Alexander had bounced back immediately when she uttered her words. His friend usually took hours to be dragged out of one of the moods that were caused by the realisation of how his life had changed. One sentence from this young woman, though, had Alexander laughing, something that happened too rarely for it to be ignored.

"Have you two met previously?" Richard asked, his curiosity piqued.

"Yes, at that disaster of a ball that you took me to three nights ago. I'm still having nightmares about that experience!" Alexander responded with a shudder.

Richard looked at the young woman, trying to place her; it was obvious she was not going to introduce herself. "Aren't you Basingstoke's niece?" he asked, finally recognising her, but he immediately became wary. If she were anything like her cousins, she would need to be given a wide berth.

"Yes," Amelia admitted reluctantly. Her cheeks burned as she correctly interpreted the expression on Mr Critchley's face. She silently cursed her aunt and cousins!

"Well, Miss Basingstoke, it is a pleasure to meet you officially. You were the shining light in an otherwise very dark evening," Alexander said. He was surprised to find out who she was, mainly because of the way her aunt had spoken to her, but he could dwell on that later. He did not have the same reservations as his friend; even on short acquaintance, he knew she was nothing like her relations.

"Thank you," Amelia said. "If you gentleman would excuse me, I need to continue my walk; the more energy Samson can use up, the quieter he is for the remainder of the day. It prevents him getting scolded by everyone he comes into contact with," she explained.

"Samson?" Alexander asked, rubbing under the dog's chin. "That's a fine name."

"He's usually referred to as 'the beast' by the staff," Amelia admitted. "Come on boy; time to go."

Amelia stepped away, but Samson did not immediately follow. The dog's hesitation gave Alexander the cue he was looking for to extend their meeting. For some reason he wanted to be in the company of the young woman; apart from Richard she was the only person who treated him like a normal human being; he did not wish her to leave quite yet.

"It seems I have a new friend Miss Basingstoke," Alexander said easily. "Would you mind if we walked with you a little way?"

"Well, of course, I don't mind, but are you sure?" Amelia said, "He might be good now, but once he starts running around, you will know his true character. Is it not better to remain in blissful ignorance of his normal behaviour? It seems he has finally lulled someone into believing he can behave himself; it would be such a shame to dispel the illusion so soon."

Alexander smiled. "I think I'd like to take the risk," he said stepping forward. Richard held out his arm, touching Alexander's elbow with his arm. Alexander used the gesture to enable him to place his hand on his friend's arm without any words being used. It was something Alexander hated doing, but it was necessary if he was to get anywhere safely.

To Amelia's utter astonishment when the group moved forward, Samson stayed at Captain Worthington's side. He walked slightly in front of the Alexander, but his body was still in contact with his leg. Amelia could hardly take her eyes off the animal; he was acting so differently than his usual boisterous self.

"You are very quiet, Miss Basingstoke; even on such short acquaintance I am used to far more from you," Alexander said as they walked.

"I'm worried that the spell you seem to have cast over Samson will soon be cast in my direction. I can think of no other reason he would be acting so out of character. He never walks to heel," Amelia responded.

"Does the thought of walking close by my side frighten you so much?" Alexander asked, teasingly.

Amelia spluttered with a laugh, "According to my aunt, I can't walk in a dignified manner. I would likely trip you and send you sprawling across the grass if I walked close to you. I'd stick with the dog if I were you. I never thought I'd say this, but he is by far the safer option."

Alexander chuckled. "In that case you are safe from my spells; today I shall concentrate on Samson alone. Although one day, I may demand that you take your turn by my side."

Richard walked without adding anything to the conversation. He was astounded but pleased. Alexander *flirting?* That was definitely a sign of improvement. It appeared that Miss Basingstoke was not as obvious as the rest of her family, but he was less inclined to trust her than Alexander seemed to be. For Richard, the family reputation made him wary. Richard felt hope for his friend though; if he could flirt with a young woman, it would not be long before he was back into the fold and being chased by the ladies.

Alexander felt that the morning was turning out to be very enjoyable. He was excessively pleased he had found out who Miss Basingstoke was; her voice had filled his thoughts for the last few nights. The chances of finding out who she was had seemed remote, particularly as he had no intention of going into Society again.

More surprising was that, with Samson walking by his side, he was experiencing a feeling of confidence. The sensation of having the dog in contact with his leg was gently reassuring, and he was walking in a far more relaxed manner than he had done since he had lost his sight. He was still holding onto Richard, but the dog was providing extra support.

They walked together until they reached the gates of the park. Alexander had been talkative all the way, something which had flustered Amelia a little and surprised Richard.

"Well, this is where I bid you good day gentlemen," Amelia said. "Now Samson, we really do have to go this time," she said firmly, putting the dog on his lead. Samson obeyed the request and returned to Amelia's side meekly.

"Thank you for your company, Miss Basingstoke," Alexander said, giving a bow. "And thank you, Samson."

Richard bowed his goodbye and led his friend onto the street, turning in the opposite direction to Miss Basingstoke. "Well, that was odd behaviour from the dog," he said. "I thought he was going to attack us when he first came bounding across the park."

"Perhaps sight loss has its advantages after all," Alexander said. "I only met a very well-behaved, gentle creature."

"Umm," Richard responded, unable to make a comment to Alexander's flippant remark.

"So, Miss Basingstoke," Alexander said when he was sure she was nowhere near. "Describe her to me."

"Why? She's nothing special, certainly not your usual type at any rate. A pleasant young lady, but with questionable relatives; that is all, really. Nothing to interest your high standards," Richard said dismissively.

"Come on, there must be something you can tell me!" Alexander said in response.

"She's not a beauty or rich. What more is there to tell?" Richard responded with a shrug of his shoulders. He had already dismissed Miss Basingstoke, just as most of the people frequenting the season had done. There was little to recommend oneself if one was lacking in beauty *and* a dowry.

Alexander frowned all the way home, frustrated at not being given a picture of the tantalising Miss Basingstoke. His 'usual' type of woman had been at pains to avoid any contact with him since his injury, something that should have made him angry but did not. He was thankful he had formed no attachments with Society's finest before Trafalgar. It would have only ended badly once he returned. It was far less painful than he would have imagined it to be to realise that he was only wanted when he was perfect in the eyes of Society and, although hailed a hero, he was now also considered tarnished goods. He was beginning to consider that he had been unfairly judgemental on people just as his old friends had been when visiting him on his return to London. It was a sobering thought and was altering the way he thought he wanted to spend the rest of his life.

# Chapter 3

Alexander's life had changed so much since his injury he sometimes wondered if his previous life had been just a dream. He had been so active, independent and alive and then the metalwork from the sail workings had exploded when the cannon ball struck, and pieces had hit him across his forehead. He had been knocked unconscious, but by that point, his ship and crew were out of danger. The cannon ball was the last one that struck his ship; he had some consolation in knowing they had fought bravely and had survived.

His eyesight was gone when he regained consciousness. His cuts had been sewn, but some metalwork remained inside. The ship's doctor, a man who had continued to tend to Alexander on his return, had been reluctant to remove it; in his opinion, the chance for survival from such an operation was slim.

Alexander had spent months with his brother, the Earl of Newton, recuperating in the countryside. The younger brother of the Earl of Newton was given every care and attention. The problem was that no matter what help was offered, Alexander was terrified about his future. He was completely dependent on others. He would no longer be able to go on a horseback ride or take command of a ship or dance. He was an invalid at seven and twenty.

The first months were filled with anger. Alexander lashed out at everyone and everything, especially when he tried to do something and failed. Family and staff learned to give him a wide birth and kept communication to a minimum. The slightest misplaced remark could cause an angry outburst.

Things were to change though. It began when Alexander had shouted at a maid and sent her scurrying from the room in tears. A few moments later his brother entered the room and slammed the door behind him.

"Alexander, we need to talk," Anthony said firmly. Anyone meeting the two brothers would immediately see the likeness they shared; both had the black hair and blue eyes of their mother.

"I'm not in the mood," Alexander responded, sullenly.

"To be honest Alex, I'm sick of your moods; so is every other person in my household."

"Sorry, but I'm not feeling sociable at the moment," Alexander replied sarcastically. "I find getting through each day takes up all of my energies."

Lord Newton sighed, "Alex, this can't go on; this is not you."

"Oh, it's me, Anthony," Alexander responded, his tone bitter. "Have you not noticed that I cannot see? Things aren't going to improve from this. The invalid before you is your brother for the rest of our lives."

"That doesn't give you the right to make everyone else's life hell. Let us help, don't push everyone away," Lord Newton appealed. He did have sympathy for his brother, but he was speaking to him knowing that things could not continue as they had so far.

"What can you do, Anthony?" Alexander said, his face showing sadness and frustration. "What can you do that will take this nightmare away? Will you help me to see again? Will you make this darkness disappear?"

"I can't do that; you know that. I would move heaven and earth if there were something I could do to give you back your sight," his brother replied with feeling. "I can help you cope with it though. I can offer support in whatever way is best. Just tell me what you need without shouting at anyone who offers help."

"I need to be left alone," Alexander responded, turning away from his brother.

Lord Newton sighed. He had hoped to reach Alexander by reasoning with him, but it was obvious that his brother was deep in a hell that was dragging him down further and affecting the whole household. It was time to leave him alone, but he would not go without one last attempt to reach his brother; he owed everyone that. "You've been raised to treat servants with respect; I expect you to treat my staff with the respect they deserve while you are a guest of mine. I'm sick of wasting time on consoling yet another hysterical maid and even a few footmen. Do not take your anger out on those who aren't in a position to fight back."

Alexander nodded his head in acquiescence. "I'm sorry; I will try not to upset them in the future."

"Thank you," Lord Newton said, rising and moving to the door. "Alex, I have always admired you. You were the brave one, the fearless one who, in my opinion, should have had the title. I always thought I was in your shadow, even though I was the eldest; but I was happy to be in that position, a little in awe of my capable brother. You may be the younger brother, but I looked up to you. I'm sorry this happened and wish that I could do something to ease your pain, but it has changed you in more ways than losing your sight."

"How?" Alexander asked, surprised but touched at his brother's words.

"It has turned you into a bitter, angry coward," Lord Newton said, rushing to say the words, preventing the opportunity for any interruption. "The Alexander I looked up to, would have faced this demon straight on. He would have done whatever it took to return to the life he enjoyed before. He would have battled every battle in order to beat this. You have rolled over and let it win; you have struck out in the most vicious way possible at anyone trying to help, punishing us all for something that none of us had any control over. The Alexander I knew would never have done that. He was better than that."

Lord Newton did not wait for a response or to see if his words had any effect. He walked out and closed the door behind him, leaving Alexander alone.

It was many minutes before Alexander calmed down after his brother's outburst. He had felt anger during the months since his injury, but nothing compared to the rage he felt at Anthony's words. As the ticking of the grandfather clock in the corner of the room passed the minutes by, Alexander finally began to breathe normally once more.

As his anger subsided, it was replaced by another emotion: shame. Anthony's words had hurt, but Alexander had to admit to himself they were truthful. He *had* acted appallingly to everyone, whether staff or family. Throughout his life, especially as he rose through the naval ranks, he had never been afraid; he was not foolhardy, but he had always had confidence in his own and his men's abilities. The problem he had now was that he no longer had a career; he had been retired from the Navy, and he lacked faith in his own ability. For the first time in his life he was frightened. Frightened of the darkness that would never go away, frightened that he would not be able to cope, frightened that he would never beat his fear.

Hours passed before Alexander finally roused himself and rang the bell for assistance. He asked for his valet to be notified that his master wished to see him, and the loyal member of staff came immediately.

"Peterson, I have a task for you to do before we leave here," Alexander started.

"Yes, Captain?" Peterson responded. Although Alexander was no longer a member of the Navy, his staff would always consider him their Captain, especially Peterson who had travelled the world with him.

"I need instructions sent to the London house in preparation for our return," Alexander said, sounding more confident than he felt.

"We're leaving?" Peterson asked, surprised. He never thought Captain Worthington would be in any fit state to return to his home.

"We are," Alexander said. "I want all the unnecessary items, the ornaments, the vases, all stored away. I want to be able to move around the house without fear of knocking over some item that my ancestors treasured. I have enough problems without being haunted by unhappy relatives."

"The parlour maid will be ecstatic," Peterson said, half to himself, but Alexander heard and chuckled at the words.

"I expect she will be. I need to sell my horses, but keep the ones for the carriage. There is no point keeping those I'm not sure I'll ever ride again. I also need people around me who will not pity me but who'll be useful," Alexander finished.

"If you tell the staff what they need to do, they will respond," Peterson said with confidence.

"At this moment Peterson, I'm not sure myself what I'll need them to do," Alexander admitted. "But I can't go on like this."

"No, sir," Peterson agreed.

"Oh, and one last thing; I'm going to give every member of staff whom I've upset a present of twenty pounds as an apology for my behaviour over these last months," Alexander said. He had behaved abominably, and it was time to make amends.

"The list could be long," Peterson said, not sure how his comment would be received but needing to make his employer aware the extent to which he had been lashing out.

"Well, if it ruins me, it will be a lesson I'll not forget so easily," Alexander said. Anthony had been correct: he never would have treated anyone so badly before; there was no excuse. It was time to change and time to fight.

*

Alexander worked hard when he returned home. He had a London residence, liking the hustle and bustle and entertainments the capital offered as any young man would. Only now did it seem the wrong place to have a residence. Rather than make the rash decision to sell and either move in with Anthony or setup a house somewhere less busy, he determined to give London life one last chance. He learned every inch of his house so he could move around confidently. It did not come easy, and there were many knocks and bruises along the way. Staff had to learn that if they moved something to clean it, it had to be replaced in exactly the same position in order to avoid a curse the next time Alexander had to move past the object. Moved objects caused unnecessary accidents.

He learned that it was easier to receive a description of where food was on a plate using a clock face as a guide, far easier than having to guess. He no longer served himself but allowed himself to be served. He accepted his glass being filled at the dining table, but he wanted some independence and solitude from his staff. He developed a knack of pouring his own drinks when in his study.

The garden was another challenge, but he faced it and eventually was confident about the pathways and seating areas.

His tailor visited the house. Alexander needed new clothes; he was no longer entitled to wear his Navy uniform. He felt a pang of remorse knowing it was something he had worn for years with pride, but he pushed the feelings to one side, cursing his vanity. Peterson was his eyes when choosing fabric for his new wardrobe, although Alexander felt every sample of material that was brought to be considered. He was determined to have some input in the process.

Throughout the challenges Alexander was facing whilst at home, he faced another hurdle during the visiting hours. It was one that he had not really expected.

On his return he received many visits. People visiting to see the hero, to find out what had happened, wanting to hear the story firsthand. It was also clear from the start that he was a freak show. The locality could come and see the blind man who could walk around his house without crashing into objects, but could not pour the tea. Once the initial visits had taken place and curiosity had been satisfied, Alexander found many whom he had considered his friends soon fell by the wayside.

He could not speak about the latest hunt or the latest beauty, so he was of little interest to the men. The women, although more pitying of his plight, no longer saw him as a possible suitor, so their interest also waned. It was not many weeks before few people visited at all, and he could not visit them in return, even if he had wanted to. Going into a strange house carried far too many risks of disaster for him to venture out.

Throughout it all Mr Richard Critchley had stood by his friend. They had been school friends, Mr Critchley coming from a rich, although untitled family. They had built up a bond that had survived Alexander's many absences because of his naval commitments.

Alexander appreciated his friend even more since his injury; Critchley was consistent, encouraging and enough of a thorn in the side to be able to drag Alexander out of his house when he thought he was up for the next challenge.

That was how Alexander had ended in a ballroom: Richard had decided Alexander needed to mix more. Richard was the optimist who would never give up hope of having back the Alexander who had existed before Trafalgar. Alexander was beginning to realise he was never going to be able to go back and, after the past few months, he was not sure he would want to if he had the choice.

# Chapter 4

Alexander was in a quandary. He wanted to go outside for a walk. Actually, if he were being honest, he wanted to spend more time in Miss Basingstoke's company *and* go for a walk with the novelty of the dog at his side. Miss Basingstoke had inadvertently given him information that was perfect; she walked the dog every morning. There was just one problem: Richard was not available every morning. He was usually only arriving home as daylight emerged, so expecting him to be ready before most people ventured into Green Park was too much. It had been a huge favour the one time Richard had accompanied him. Alexander had needed to feel the open air and, although Richard had complained bitterly about the hour, he had escorted his friend. Alexander could not have faced the park when it was time for everyone to promenade.

Alexander also had the suspicion that Richard might not have been keen if he realised Alexander wanted to pursue Miss Basingstoke. Alexander had not pushed his friend when he had dismissed the request to describe the lady, but he was sure part of the reason for Richard's dismissal was because of the family she was connected to. Anyone of sense would be wary around a relative of Lady Basingstoke, but Alexander was drawn to the young lady. She was the only person he had met, apart from Richard, who had treated him like an intelligent human being; she had made silly remarks and did not fall over herself in trying to avoid the topic of his sight loss. She had been *normal*, and he longed for contact with people who said what they thought rather than what they presumed was expected, which were empty words. The worst thing about his situation was the loneliness and the lack of interaction with people other than his servants.

The problem was reaching her. He did not want to pay her household a visit; that would put him in Lady Basingstoke's clutches, and he wanted to avoid contact with Miss Serena Basingstoke at all cost. He had to find a way of walking in Green Park when it was likely she would be there.

He eventually decided that Peterson would be a suitable replacement for Richard. The ever loyal valet escorted his master without complaint even though the air was crisp and the ground still slightly icy at such an early hour. They walked along the lanes in the park for three days before he heard Miss Basingstoke's shouts and heard the thudding of Samson running across the ground. Peterson stiffened as the dog approached.

Alexander just had the opportunity to say, "Don't worry," before the dog came to a stop before them. "Good morning, Samson," Alexander addressed the dog.

The words were the cue the dog needed. He moved around Alexander as he had done the first time, pushing between Peterson and Alexander before moving to Alexander's left side. He received the scratch on his neck that he seemed to like and sat down, patiently waiting for Amelia to catch up.

"Samson!" Amelia said, gasping for breath as she reached the group. "I'm sorry! He was so far away from me. I had no idea it was you when he started running."

"Did you miss me, boy?" Alexander said, scratching the dog's head.

"He certainly looks pleased to see you," Peterson said, eyeing the dog warily.

"He won't harm you," Amelia assured the valet. "He's too boisterous, but there's no real harm in him."

"I'm sure that's what all owners say," Peterson sniffed. "I'd prefer it if he was kept on a lead."

"Peterson, don't be so mistrusting!" Alexander teased his employee. "He's as gentle as a lamb."

"A lamb of giant proportions and large teeth," Peterson responded, not afraid to say what he was thinking.

Amelia laughed. "He's never been likened to a lamb before! He isn't vicious though; truly he has never inflicted anything but slobber on anyone, which I admit, isn't always welcome," she assured the valet.

"Well, Miss Basingstoke, we have not seen you for a few days; have you been neglecting Samson?" Alexander asked.

Amelia felt pleased that her presence in the park had been missed but quickly suppressed the feeling; there was no use letting herself get carried away. He was out of her reach, blind or not blind. "I was needed to help my aunt, so I was unable to take him on our usual walk. The poor thing had to make do with a short walk around the square in which we live."

"Well, Samson, I too am disappointed. I missed your support as I walked," Alexander said to the dog. "May we join you once again Miss Basingstoke? I found the feeling of Samson against my leg to be a reassuring sensation as we walked last time."

"Certainly," Amelia responded, smiling to herself. It was a good thing she had not become carried away with Alexander's first words. He had missed the dog, not her. "I can't promise he will do the same though."

Samson proved Amelia wrong. He stayed by Alexander's side as they walked, again placing himself a little to the front of his body. Alexander rested his hand on the dog's neck, and they walked comfortably together. The position was possible because of the size of the dog; he was a large creature, and Alexander's hand rested naturally on his neck.

"He's never done anything like this before," Amelia mused as they walked.

"Perhaps he senses I need the help," Alexander responded.

"But you don't, really," Amelia countered. "You have the support of the person who is walking with you."

"Perhaps he thinks he can do a better job?" Alexander asked, laughing when Peterson harrumphed at his side.

"Probably. He always thinks he's the best at everything," Amelia said with a smile. "Uncle Jeremy said he refused to seek the birds when he took him shooting. He swore that Samson looked at him with disgust and lay down as if to say he was far too good for such a task. He would have sold him, only he was worthless in the eyes of any who had seen him in action. Poor Uncle Jeremy."

"Poor Samson," Alexander defended his new friend. "I would rather have him by my side than wasting his time searching for dead birds."

As they walked Alexander felt he could not ask anything other than the usual pleasantries even though he really wanted to find out more about the young lady who walked with him. It was not appropriate to ask the questions he wanted to while Peterson was in company with them and so close. He trusted his valet not to gossip, but his presence made things so much more uncomfortable, so he could not ask further personal questions. Alexander still needed to rest his arm on the valet's as another measure of support. Alexander cursed his blindness again; would there be no privacy in his future?

When they reached the gate where they had previously separated, Alexander was struck with inspiration. "Miss Basingstoke, could I ask something of you?"

"Yes, of course," Amelia responded while attaching the lead to the dog.

"Samson seems to look on me as someone he needs to help. If we met at these gates tomorrow, would you mind if I accompanied you without my valet's support and just walked with the dog?" Alexander was taking a risk. Although the dog had supported him twice, there was no guarantee he would continue to do so. If he ran off in the middle of Green Park, Miss Basingstoke would be obliged to chase after him, potentially leaving Alexander alone in the middle of a wide open space. By taking this chance, though, Alexander would be outside without support for the first time since his injury, and he would also be in the company of a lady who he wanted to get to know a little better.

Amelia seemed to be having the same doubts and hesitated when responding. "I realise he has been very well behaved the two times you have met, but—"

"I will not place any recriminations on you or the dog should he behave differently. I promise if you need to chase him, I shall remain stock still until you can come and rescue me," Alexander reassured her. He was drawn to the young lady without doubt but, once he had thought of the idea, it seemed like an attractive one. It would be interesting to see how it felt to walk with just the dog leading the way.

Amelia sighed. "I think you will be disappointed, but I will meet you here tomorrow, if you wish." She could not refuse to meet the captain. Spending time in his company could rapidly become the highlight of her day.

"Thank you." Alexander bowed. "I shall look forward to tomorrow."

"You may regret those words," Amelia muttered but smiled at Alexander's laugh as he walked away with his valet. "You'd better not let him down, Samson," she instructed the dog, ruffling the fur on his head as she tugged his lead.

*

Alexander had arranged with Peterson that he should wait on the first bench they came to in the park. Although once out of sight he would be of no practical use, Alexander needed his valet to escort him to and from the park. If Samson did not behave, Alexander would have to stand still until rescued, but he had no intention of keeping in sight of his valet. The thought of being free even for a short time made his heart pound in anticipation; in addition, his mood was lightened at the thought of being accompanied by a young lady. He had missed female company, and that Miss Basingstoke seemed intelligent and witty only added to her attraction.

Amelia was waiting at the gates for Alexander. She had set out even earlier than normal to let Samson get rid of his first burst of energy. Standing at the gate she could appreciate the sight of Alexander walking down the street. Even with his reliance on someone to lead him he walked upright. His shoulders were back and his strides long. He dwarfed the valet when in fact there were not too many inches difference in height. It was the way Alexander held himself that made him appear to tower over Peterson. He no longer wore the uniform of the Navy, but he looked magnificent in a deep blue frock coat, buckskin breeches and gleaming boots. He was a devastatingly handsome man in Amelia's eyes. She smiled as the gentlemen approached, her smile growing when Samson woofed gently and wagged his tail at his new friend's approach.

"Well, Samson, I hope that greeting is a good sign," Alexander said cheerfully. The dog circled him, as he had done previously and sat at his side, his tail thumping the ground. "Shall we start, Miss Basingstoke?"

"Whenever you are ready," Amelia said. She started to walk, and Samson and Alexander joined her, Samson keeping pace with her. She was a little reserved; she had been with other people when in Alexander's company until now. All of a sudden, who she was with seemed to daunt her. He felt huge as he walked by her side, which was foolish, as she had sat next to him only two weeks ago. She cursed herself and shook her head, trying to dismiss her nonsensical thoughts; it did not make conversation easier for her. She was for the first time in her life tongue-tied.

"Could you describe Samson to me?" Alexander asked. He was also quite nervous, although it had more to do with being reliant on Samson, but he would never have admitted disquiet, and asking for description was always a good way to settle his nerves. If he could picture something in his mind's eye, he felt more reassured.

"Apart from large, uncontrollable brute, you mean?" Amelia replied with a grin.

"We've already established that we disagree on that score," Alexander responded with an easy smile and a ruffle of Samson's head.

"I don't agree with his detractors actually," Amelia confessed. "I'll try to describe him, although this feels a little strange. His coat is golden; you can probably feel how it grows in long curls," she started. "His eyes are my favourite part of him; they are almost black and seem to laugh, especially when he is about to do something mischievous."

"He's obviously intelligent," Alexander added.

"Yes. When he's happy, his tongue lolls out of the left side of his mouth. I don't know why, but it's always the left."

"Is his tongue lolling now?" Alexander asked quickly.

"Yes," Amelia reassured him, smiling at the uncertainty in his voice. "As soon as he sees you, the tongue comes out."

"I'm glad." When few friends existed, Alexander needed to keep hold of the ones around him, even if one was a four-legged creature of dubious character.

"He has the bushiest tail," Amelia continued. "I'm sure if he had chased the birds, it would have become tangled in the undergrowth, but it is nice to feel it pounding against your leg when he's walking along. That's it really; you know about his personality traits although you have only seen the best of him so far."

"The 'so far' does worry me a little, but he is doing very well. I cannot express how good it feels to be able to walk along without being attached to someone," Alexander said with feeling.

"It must be hard going from complete independence to total reliance on others," Amelia said. Her voice was sympathetic but not pitying.

"You cannot imagine how hard," came the quiet reply. They walked in silence for a few moments. "Tell me about yourself, Miss Basingstoke. I know nothing of you."

Amelia flushed and was grateful that her embarrassment could not be seen. It was easier to be confident when the man you had admired since you had first seen him three seasons ago could not see you. "There is very little to tell," she said dismissively.

"Said like a modest miss. I would have expected more from you," Alexander teased. "I know nothing about your family."

Amelia was once again reminded that they would never have crossed paths if it were not for the injury. She sighed quietly; she needed to keep that fact in her mind so her foolish heart could not run away with itself. Nothing could stop her enjoying his company though. "I am somewhere in the middle of nine children," she started. "I'm the only girl. I think I was spoiled and bullied in equal measure by my brothers."

Alexander laughed. "Eight brothers? Woe betide anyone who tries to take liberties with you; they would have sixteen fists to fight off!"

"If I were the beauty of the season, that might be so, but since I'm a confirmed wallflower, I think the gentlemen of our social circle are safe," Amelia countered. She did not mind his teasing; she could take what he said in the spirit in which it was offered.

"The fact that you have eight brothers lurking in the background may have put off one or two gentlemen. Are all your brothers in London?"

"No, the eldest two are settled near home, both farming the land. With the next two, one is in the Navy and one is studying to take Orders; we hope he will find a living close to home. Of my younger brothers, the two youngest are still at school; then I have one who is an apprentice printer and one who is an apprentice in a solicitor's office. We are very proud of them all." Amelia's tone was a little defensive; she was fully aware of what the *ton* thought of anyone who earned a living outside the military or clergy. They were the only professions not met with derision.

Alexander had picked up her tone. He had been surprised at her answer; her being connected to Sir Jeremy Basingstoke, he had assumed she came from a higher ranking family than it appeared she did. "Your parents must be very pleased with all their family," he said. "What vessel is your brother serving on?"

Amelia smiled; it was obvious the Captain would be most interested in the brother who was serving in the Navy. "He's serving on board the HMS Agamemnon," she replied.

"A ship that was Nelson's favourite," Alexander said. "Although in my opinion it hasn't been the best of ships."

"Why?" Amelia was alarmed for her brother.

"Oh nothing that should worry you," Alexander reassured her. "She ran aground in Copenhagen and has always seemed to need some sort of repair. She probably would have been scrapped if we hadn't gone back to war."

"And constantly needing repair is supposed to calm my worry?" Amelia asked.

Alexander chuckled. "We look after our ships; they are as precious as the crew, in many cases more so. Did he serve at Trafalgar?"

"He did," Amelia said quietly. "His letters were jolly, but he couldn't hide some of the horror he'd seen."

"No battle is easy for anyone, let alone a young boy," Alexander acknowledged. "What rank is he?"

"Able Seaman at the moment, but he has hopes of becoming a Petty Officer soon," Amelia said proudly.

"If he works hard he will achieve that rank and more," Alexander said. "The Navy is the one place where hard work is rewarded. I hope he does well; it's a fine career to have. How long have you been with your uncle?" Alexander needed to change the subject. A lump appeared in his chest every time he was reminded of what he had lost. He felt as if he had been born to be in the navy, and it never failed to leave him struggling for breath when he realised that life had disappeared forever.

"This will be my third season. I'm glad to say it will be my last," Amelia responded with feeling.

"Really?" Alexander did not know whether or not he was surprised she was glad to be returning home or that they had not met during her first season. Admittedly, he had been missing for most of the last season.

"Yes, I'll soon be three and twenty, time to return home and establish my life there. Staying with my uncle has been a diversion but cannot continue indefinitely," Amelia tried to sound grateful about staying with her uncle and his family, but the reality was that she would be glad to leave London.

She was two and twenty and yet she had attended only two seasons. The reality of her family's position hit home to Alexander and something else as well. He felt himself colour and was hopeful she would not notice it. He would not have met her during her previous seasons because she would have belonged to the group of people he would have considered beneath his notice. He would not have been rude to anyone, oh no, not the great Captain Worthington, but he would not have sought out any lady's hand in that group either. He felt shame that he was now willing, no desperate, for her company when, if he still had sight, he would not have sought her out at all.

"I am genuinely sorry our paths did not cross sooner," Alexander said quietly. He meant the words, although he was still battling with feelings of shame at the reflection of his own character. He recalled the words she had first used to describe him.

"Oh, you had your friends; I had benches to polish. We were both busy," Amelia said flippantly, but she had noticed his flush. They were both intelligent and knew full well why their paths had not crossed, and it made her heart sink a little. The *ton* were never willing to step outside their closed group unless the money of the lower classes was needed, of course. She was realistic. It offered no flattery to her that he wanted to be in her company; her dog was the bigger attraction.

Samson had behaved impeccably throughout the walk. Amelia had taken them on a circular route in order to eventually return to the valet. She was thankful when she saw his form on the bench. Needing to be prepared for the catastrophe that could happen if Samson misbehaved had kept her on edge, but being reminded of her true position in society had come as an unwelcome jolt to her.

"We are returning to your valet," Amelia informed him. "We have reached the end of our excursion."

Alexander could have cursed that they were approaching Peterson. He wanted to say more, to rectify something that had gone wrong during their walk, but now he could not. Amelia stopped and, when Peterson stood and offered his arm to his master, Amelia called Samson to her. The dog must have sensed something amiss in the mood between the couple, as he meekly left Alexander and sat before Amelia.

"Miss Basingstoke, I cannot express how much the walk and the sense of freedom this morning has meant," Alexander said with feeling. He did not want to end their contact, but he knew the atmosphere that now existed between them was as a result of them both realising why they had never before been introduced. The reality of social interaction in London had prevented it and, in many respects, Alexander's own arrogant attitude.

"You're welcome," Amelia responded. "Samson certainly seemed to enjoy it."

"Am I asking too much for us to walk again?" Alexander asked. He did not want it to be the only time he experienced freedom, but it was more than that; he wanted a chance for them to return to easy terms. Her good opinion of him was suddenly very important to him.

Amelia hesitated; she, of course, wanted to spend time in Alexander's company; she had been aware of him since the first time she had seen him in a ballroom, during that first season. The problem was that, the more she saw of him and spoke to him, the more difficult it would be to forget him when it was time to return home. And forgetting him would be her only option when she returned to her family.

"I'm not sure—," she started, but was interrupted.

"Please," Alexander said quietly.

He might no longer meet the eyes of the person he was communicating with, but his expression was no less beseeching for the lack of the usual interaction. "I shall be waiting here at the same time tomorrow," Amelia said, dismissing her sensible side. His request was heartfelt; she could not refuse him.

Chapter 5

A breath of relief whooshed out of Alexander when he heard the gentle 'woof' of Samson. He had not been sure Miss Basingstoke would attend even though she had given her agreement. During the previous evening when he had reflected on their conversation, he acknowledged that he had pressured her into meeting. All night he had been worried that she would have second thoughts, and he would have no further contact with her. He had convinced himself it was the freedom of being with Samson he was desperate for; thoughts of anything else would only cause more fear and doubt, and he could not face that just yet.

"Good morning, Miss Basingstoke, Samson," Alexander said, sounding more confident than he was. He felt calmer when Samson automatically took his place at his side, and he was able to scratch the neck of the furry animal. He felt Samson's tail flicking at his legs as it swished from side to side, and he could picture the dog's tongue lolling from the side of his mouth.

"Good morning," Amelia responded. She was smiling but once again was a little nervous.

"Can we take a different route from the one we took yesterday?" Alexander asked, keen to start their walk. "If you could describe the paths we are walking along, I might recognise where we are."

"Of course," Amelia agreed easily. She started to walk as she had done previously, but this time she described what she saw. What trees were around them, the paths they followed and which direction they were heading along with any of the seating areas or ornamental statues they passed. "This feels a little strange," Amelia admitted as she walked.

"Walking with me?" Alexander asked.

"No!" Amelia smiled. "Describing objects and places in the parkland I think you might recognise. I need to think of words that will describe it without using the flowery language one would be expected to use when talking about an object of art or a painting. Explaining the reality rather than concentrating on the picturesque."

"You are doing very well. I can't describe how frustrating it is to hear a different sound and have no clue what it relates to."

"It must make you feel very vulnerable," Amelia said quietly.

"It does, but I'm trying to accustom myself to the sense of being in the dark in more ways than one." The wry smile that followed Alexander's words pulled at Amelia's heart. She did not feel sorry for him but wanted to make things better.

Alexander listened to everything being said and, when he was sure of his location, he interrupted the flow of commentary. "We must be just around the corner from the huge copper beech tree," he said, almost sure he knew where he was.

"That's right," Amelia said.

"There's a small opening with seating nearby, isn't there?" Alexander asked.

"Yes."

"Would you mind if we sat for a moment?" Alexander asked. With Amelia's agreement, he asked her to stop. "I'm going to try something with Samson."

"Oh?" Amelia was immediately a little wary. "Don't forget Samson has never been so good for so long, so testing him may not turn out well," she said cautiously.

"Don't worry, it's only an idea of mine; it doesn't matter if it fails. It was only when I was thinking about our walk yesterday that I realised something," Alexander explained, keen to share his idea with her. "You never gave Samson an instruction as to whether we were turning left or right along any of the paths we took."

"No, I didn't, but he could see my movements; I was walking alongside you," Amelia said, not sure where the conversation was going.

"Yes, but it was only as I returned to my home with Peterson that I realised something. Samson had been putting gentle pressure on my leg. Unbeknown to me, he was guiding my steps in the right direction. It was only when he was no longer next to me I realised what he'd done," Alexander said excitedly. It was true; he had missed the pressure when it was no longer there. He was not sure whether it was something Samson had done unconsciously or consciously. One thing he was certain of was that he felt more confident with the dog at his side.

"I think it might have been just a coincidence," Amelia said doubtfully. She had always been Samson's biggest defender, but even she realised the dog had his limitations.

"Please humour me in this," Alexander requested. "If you will lead the way, I'll keep repeating 'seat' to him. I'm not expecting it to work today, but I hope that, if we try it every day, he may learn the command," Alexander explained.

Amelia turned to walk towards the seat, and Samson followed her lead. Alexander was all the time saying "Seat, Samson. Seat, Samson." They reached the bench, and Alexander made a huge fuss of Samson, even bringing a treat for him out of his pocket.

"That's the perfect way to reward him; he will love you forever if you feed him treats every day," Amelia laughed as Samson wolfed down the treat in one bite and then pushed his nose into Alexander's hand, just to make sure he had eaten everything on offer.

"He deserves it; I really cannot explain how good it is not to have to hold onto someone all the time. I know you are there in case something goes wrong, but I feel confident with him. It doesn't feel as if he'll run away," Alexander tried to explain.

"It must have been hard to have to learn to accept help. I can't imagine it came naturally to you," Amelia said, being bolder than she should have been.

Alexander laughed slightly, "My brother thankfully took me to task when I was punishing everyone who tried to help."

"He's a brave man," Amelia said. "I've seen your glowers when people got in the way." It was true that she thought him the most handsome man she had ever seen, but she was under no illusion of his character; she had seen him send people scuttling away with one of his glares.

Alexander was reminded of what she had said on his first meeting with her. "You must have had a low opinion of my behaviour in the past."

Amelia flushed; she could not be honest with him. What would she say? That I thought you the most attractive man in any ballroom I visited? That despite your faults you made my heart beat a little faster every time I saw you? No, she might talk to him in a way she would not consider with anyone else, but in this she could not be so forward. Even now as he sat on the bench, he was a fine figure of a man; he sat upright, slightly leaning forwards, his hands on each of his knees as if ready to spring into action at any time. "I sometimes speak before I think; in fact, I often do it. Ignore what I said when we first met; I was being flippant, and it was very rude of me."

"Hmm, I think you were being truthful. My brother would say as much if asked," Alexander admitted. "I'd never thought of myself the way you or Anthony described me, but I've had to face up to a lot these past months. Reflecting on my behaviour has not been a pleasant experience, but necessary if I was to deal with the sight loss and start living again."

"I think you've had enough to deal with without having to change your personality as well," Amelia defended him.

"Would it make sense if I said I'm glad the change took place?" Alexander asked. "Oh, don't get me wrong; I wasn't at the start, and I think I still struggle more times than I handle what I face. I can't shake off the thought, though, that if I'd died and all I left in the minds of people who did not know me well was that I was stiff lipped, glowering and reserved, I'd feel saddened they had not seen my true character."

"Will you ever let me forget those words?" Amelia said with embarrassment.

"Probably not," Alexander said with a smile that lit up his face. Amelia caught her breath; he was handsome even when he did not smile, but when he smiled, his whole face brightened with amusement and, for the first time in her life, she felt breathless.

He held out his hand and, although Amelia hesitated, she placed her own in his. Alexander squeezed her gloved fingers; they felt small in his own large hand. It was the first physical contact they had shared, and it gave him an idea of her size. She was obviously slightly built, her hand small and slender. He felt bolder than he would have in different circumstances. He allowed his free hand to roam across her fingers and down to her wrist. He was pleased when he heard the slight intake of breath. It was the first positive response from a woman he had experienced in over a year, and it took a lot of strength for him to gather himself. The last thing he needed was to push her too far, insult her and be left alone on a bench in the middle of Green Park.

He took a deep breath and pulled himself together; he had never been one to take advantage of an innocent girl, and he certainly was not going to start now. "Miss Basingstoke, please be assured that I'm not ignorant of the debt I owe you."

Amelia flushed a deep red, and her heart raced; his grip felt strong and sure, but when he used his other hand to examine her clasped one, she needed all her willpower to prevent herself from leaning into him. She had never been a weak and feeble miss, but his touch almost turned her into one.

"There's no need to thank me; I'm happy to be here," she said, her voice a little softer than usual. It was true; she was happy to be with him. She was also foolish and silly, she silently cursed to herself, shaking her idiotic thoughts away.

Alexander squeezed her hand before releasing it. "You shouldn't dismiss what you've done for me. I wish there was something I could do for you in return."

"You could find a ship that could spirit my aunt and cousin away perhaps?" Amelia said flippantly.

"Are they so bad?" Alexander asked. Their reputation had been enough to keep him at such a distance that he could not claim a detailed knowledge of them or their ways.

"They have been very good in giving me a home these past few seasons, it's just—I miss the country and my family," Amelia responded. It was not polite to seem ungrateful about her relations to someone who was almost a stranger.

"Yes, I can understand that," Alexander responded, not pushing her for further information. It would not have been polite to do so, although it was clear she was unhappy with her relatives. He had felt her body stiffen as it had on the first night he had met her just before her aunt had made her presence felt. "It must be a huge change from your home life."

"It is; there is a lot more freedom in the country while every move is watched and commented upon in town. I'm glad I'm not important enough to attract much attention, but even so I have to be careful. It's stifling!" Amelia said with feeling. The attention her aunt and cousin attracted was far too much for her liking. Everyone seemed to watch their every move; it was all to prevent Serena getting her way and compromising some poor gentleman, of course, but it did not make life comfortable for those around them. Amelia pushed thoughts of her relatives aside. "You must miss the sea." Her words were a statement rather than a question. She knew enough of her companion to know he must be suffering in ways that exceeded the physical.

"I do," Alexander said quietly. No one had ever mentioned the sea to him; none had seemed to understand its importance in his life. "Every day I long to visit the ocean again, but I'm not sure I ever will."

"I know you wouldn't be able to see it," Amelia started, correctly interpreting Alexander's reluctance. "But you would be able to hear it and smell it. Although I am far away from the sea now, I can never forget the sound of the waves on the pebbles, or the smell that is so different from anything else. I'm fascinated with the crying of seagulls and the way they circle the fishing boats coming into the harbour."

"I never sleep very well on land. I seem to need to hear the sound of the waves to have a deep, restful night. I've always said the waves rock me to sleep, but it's more than that," Alexander said. He had turned, leaning back on the seat, stretching his legs out in front of him. An outsider would think he was totally relaxed because of his posture, but Amelia saw the frown and knew he was hurting deep inside. His injury had taken away more than his sight.

"I can't imagine how you have the strength to face each day; you are braver than people realise," Amelia said gently.

Alexander harrumphed. "My brother would disagree; he had to take me to task before I started behaving like a gentleman instead of the beast I'd turned into."

"Well, that's all in the past now," Amelia said, wanting to carry on the conversation but rousing herself; they had sat still too long. It was not appropriate for them to remain seated without a chaperone. She might not mind anyone seeing her walking with Samson unchaperoned, but being caught on a bench with a gentleman would put them both in line for conjecture on their relationship. "Come, let's see if Samson will return you to the seat if we walk a little away."

Alexander stood and immediately Samson moved to his usual position on the left side of him. "Right boy, lead on," Alexander said. The dog seemed to understand and walked forward with Alexander. Amelia followed but was holding back a little; she was interested to notice that the dog did not seem to be waiting for her direction.

When they had walked a distance from the bench they had just vacated, Alexander stopped and turned slightly, facing the way they had just walked. Samson remained by his side.

Alexander scratched the dog's neck. "Come on, boy; I know you can do it," he whispered. Standing straight, he said in a louder voice, "Samson, seat. Samson, seat."

The dog started to move forward with Alexander saying the same words over and over again. The journey was slow; Alexander was hesitant, and Samson seemed to sense the fear and nerves Alexander was facing, so he walked slower than he normally did.

Amelia was watching the dog closely as the pair walked. He was obviously happy, his tail wagging, although slower than it normally did. Every time Alexander spoke, Samson glanced up at him, cocking his ears. She could see the concentration and frown on Alexander's face. Forcing herself to hang back, she willed Samson to perform well.

After what seemed like an age, Alexander felt Samson stop, and then felt the hard ironwork of the bench. He reached out to feel the structure and then turned to Samson, "Good boy! Good boy!" he said, ruffling the dog's fur, making a real fuss of him. "What an excellent fellow! Good boy!"

Amelia joined the pair, laughing and reaching over to stroke Samson. "He did it! Well done, Samson," she said, relieved that he had behaved impeccably.

"Miss Basingstoke, you have an amazing animal," Alexander said, flushed with the pleasure of having achieved something without the help of another person.

"There are many who would disagree with that statement but, at this moment, I cannot," Amelia conceded. She had an idea why Alexander was so full of praise, and it choked her a little. He had achieved a walk to a specified place in the open air with only Samson for help. It must have been liberating. "But I'm afraid I need to take Samson back now. We have been out longer than we normally are."

Alexander's face fell, "Oh of course, I was being selfish. Will you be able to meet me tomorrow?" he asked, wanting to keep the feeling of elation and anticipation on what else they could teach Samson.

"I will try my best," Amelia said. "We will be going to another ball tonight, but I expect not to be overtired from too much dancing."

The words were said in jest, but Alexander detected a note of wistfulness in her tone. "My acquaintances are fools, but their loss is my gain, Miss Basingstoke. I would miss our morning outings if they ceased."

Amelia knew the compliment was aimed at Samson, mainly, but she did not argue. It did not really matter; she had the benefit of spending time in the company of a very handsome, interesting man. She would have to give Samson a huge treat when they returned; he had worked hard.

They walked back to Peterson with Alexander trying to describe the feelings of nerves and elation he had felt. He was animated and full of smiles, which made Amelia smile with pleasure. The walk seemed too short before she had to say her goodbyes and attach Samson to his lead. He was quiet on the journey home; Amelia wondered if concentrating wore him out as much as a good run did.

She left Samson with the staff after persuading cook to allow him a large bone. Samson had immediately settled down on his blanket with the unexpected treat, his tail thudding the stone floor whenever anyone looked at him; he had no intention of moving until the bone had been devoured.

Amelia returned to the main house and approached the wooden staircase. She needed to change her dress in order to be available for whatever tasks her aunt had planned for her. Not really concentrating on what she was doing, she almost collided with Serena, who was descending the stairs.

"Watch where you're going!" Serena snapped, shrilly.

"Sorry, I was distracted," Amelia apologised.

"Your boots are a disgrace; have you been walking that hound again?" Serena looked with derision at Amelia's attire.

"Yes, he settles down if I exercise him. It's better for him and the staff," Amelia explained patiently. She was not about to explain that the last few days, life had been better for herself as well.

"I find it novel that you put the needs of an animal and staff above your own appearance. It's no wonder everyone gives you a wide berth; you probably smell of dog, the amount of time you spend with him," Serena sneered.

"Rather that, than everyone giving me a wide berth because they are terrified I will trick them into marriage," Amelia snapped back.

Serena flushed with anger, "I'll be glad when you can return to your penniless hole at the end of the season," she snarled.

"Not as glad as I will be; I'm counting the days!" Amelia retorted and walked around her cousin. She did not usually let her feelings get the better of her, but she was not about to let Serena get away with her remarks. Amelia would have had a far better time without the curse of being related to her aunt and cousin. She probably would not have received any marriage offers, a girl without a dowry who was also not a great beauty would hardly be at the top of any potential suitor's list, but she might have had a few more acquaintances and, as a result, dances.

When she changed her pelisse and outdoor dress into her plain muslin day dress her afternoon was spent as it always was: at the beck and call of her aunt. It was obvious that Serena had reported what Amelia had said to her because the cutting remarks from her aunt were at an all-time high. It was a relief when Amelia was forbidden to go to the ball on a trumped up excuse; she was able to go to bed at a reasonable time, looking forward to her morning appointment.

Chapter 6

Amelia and Samson both hurried to the park as planned. Amelia still arrived earlier than the appointed time to enable Samson to run off some energy before they met Alexander. After yesterday's events Amelia was keen to see what the day would bring. She was trying to convince herself that she was helping Alexander as any good Samaritan would, rather than feeling excitement at the thought of spending an hour in a handsome man's company.

She might not have been so happy if she had known in which direction Alexander's thoughts were leaning. He had sat for most of the evening, trying to work out how he could use Samson to help him. He had started to think beyond the meeting every day; he wanted to spend a lot more time with the dog. He wanted to own him. The possibilities of having a dog that could guide him by using simple instructions was opening the world like nothing else had done since the battle. People would think him eccentric using a dog as a guide, but he was happy with that if it meant he gained some freedom.

There was one problem he had to think through: he could not just go banging on the Basingstoke's door and ask to buy the dog; they would consider it odd behaviour. Apart from that, it would put Miss Basingstoke in a difficult position and put him in the way of Miss Serena Basingstoke, something he wanted to avoid at all costs. He would have to think carefully about his next step.

Alexander heard Samson's welcoming 'woof' as he was guided to the gate as usual; he smiled at the dog. "Good morning. I hope you are both well?"

Amelia could not stop the wry smile that spread across her face. "It's the first time I've shared equal status with a dog," she said pleasantly. "It's a good thing Samson is my favourite animal."

Alexander laughed. "I'm no good at flattery, am I?"

"I don't think Samson would have any complaints," Amelia said easily.

She released Samson, and he immediately walked to Alexander's left side. "Shall we, Miss Basingstoke?" Alexander asked, keen to continue with the work they had started the previous day.

"Lead on," Amelia said. She did not think Alexander realised just how confident he was when Samson was in position. She would always be worried that Samson would be distracted, but as each day passed, it seemed to be a less likely occurrence.

Amelia followed the pair, keeping slightly behind. Samson was taking the route they had taken the day before, using his body to gently guide Alexander. She only interrupted the walk when they were approaching the bench they had used the day before.

"I think Samson is looking forward to his treats; we're already at the bench," she said.

"Good boy!" Alexander said and started to repeat the training of asking Samson to seek out the seat.

After Samson responded flawlessly, Amelia interrupted. "Perhaps if we move further along to a different seat, we can test if Samson understands the word 'seat', or if it is just this particular bench that he associates with treats," she suggested.

"Excellent thought!" Alexander said easily. "If you wouldn't mind leading us to one that you think is a suitable challenge? Lead on, Samson."

Amelia picked a stone seat rather than another iron one, and Alexander started saying his command. To both parties' delight, Samson performed perfectly. After ten minutes, Alexander remained on the seat instead of immediately standing and trying moving away to repeat the action. "You have relieved me of all the treats Samson. Well done boy!"

"He's been outstanding," Amelia admitted, taking the place next to Alexander but not sitting too close.

"Well, while we let him bathe in our worship, tell me about the ball you attended," Alexander said.

"Oh, I didn't attend after all," Amelia replied, distractedly stroking Samson as he settled between them.

"You didn't attend? Why ever not?" Alexander asked. Then he was struck with a thought. "It wasn't because of the early hour we meet was it?" He would be mortified if his needs had prevented her enjoying a ball.

"No, not at all!" Amelia said quickly. Her tone betrayed her discomfort; she did not wish to lie, but felt disloyal at criticising her family, no matter how exasperating they were.

"Why did you not go?" Alexander demanded, his laughter gone. He was quick to pick up on the uncomfortable tone in her voice.

"It was nothing," Amelia said. "Shall we continue our walk?"

"Miss Basingstoke, I would never have expected anything from you but complete honesty. From our first meeting you have said exactly what you think. I'm disappointed you don't regard me enough to tell me the truth," Alexander said, showing the glower that Amelia had seen so often the previous season.

"It's not that," Amelia said defensively. She sighed. "I don't want to tell you because I'd have to reveal more of my family than I would wish to be public knowledge."

"Tell me," Alexander said, but his tone was gentle.

"I upset my aunt yesterday, so she forbade me from attending the ball," Amelia admitted.

"What could you have possibly done that would result in that punishment?" Alexander asked astounded. He wondered how Lady Basingstoke could treat her niece as if she were a naughty schoolchild instead of the young lady that she was.

Amelia laughed a little. "I did not embroider her handkerchief to the standard she required," Amelia said with a shrug. "It was nothing; I didn't mind. There was no chance that my presence was missed; I did not disappoint any gentlemen by my absence." Her words were said lightly, but they could not fully hide the slight hurt in her voice.

"I'm sorry," Alexander said.

"What for?" Amelia asked.

"For not finding you that ship to send your relatives away," Alexander replied, but he had reached out his hand.

Amelia instinctively put her hand in his and gasped when Alexander immediately put her hand to his lips and kissed it. She might be wearing gloves, but she felt the pressure of his lips and blushed furiously. She laughed a little to try to break the serious air that had descended on them.

Alexander smiled. "That's the first time I've ever made a young lady laugh by kissing her hand!"

"And have there been many young ladies?" Amelia asked archly.

"Far too many to count. Everyone loves a man of His Majesty's Navy," Alexander said, puffing out his chest.

"Oh, I know; I saw the crowds flocking around you during my first season!" Amelia said, betraying that she had watched him.

"The crowds that disappeared the moment I was not the perfect specimen?" Alexander said with a sneer.

"Well, Samson and I have benefited from their absence," Amelia said with feeling.

"I'd much rather have your company than theirs," Alexander said honestly.

Amelia suppressed the thought that, if things had been the same, he would never have been in her company. "Thank you, but Samson will be getting bored; let's move," she said, standing.

They continued their walk, the first few moments in silence. "Does Sir Jeremy never take Samson out?" Alexander asked.

"No. He says that he would get rid of him, except he would lose money," Amelia said. "I would miss him, though; he is the nicest person in the house."

Alexander felt a pang of guilt, but pushed it aside. "I rate Samson highly, but it's a sorry state of affairs if he is your favourite. Do your parents know you are unhappy?"

"Oh no!" Amelia said. "I would never be so ungrateful as to complain about the opportunity they arranged for me. I have enjoyed some of my time in London; it has been an experience I will never forget."

"Probably for all the wrong reasons," Alexander said drily and was rewarded with a quiet laugh.

"It's unfair to make me admit how flawed my relations are," Amelia said, still smiling. "Most people I meet would consider them perfect in comparison to my own. My brothers have occupations and would not be approved of."

"I know. We are all fools," Alexander responded, including himself in his condemnation. He had been a fool in the past, dismissing people because of their rank or lack of it. His two most helpful, supportive, compassionate friends were both untitled.

"I can't argue with you on that point," Amelia responded, happy when Alexander grinned at her. He was even more handsome when he smiled, but the boyish grin made her stomach twist and her breath catch. For the first time in her life, she wished she had a dowry or something that would have attracted someone like Captain Worthington. She shook herself and smiled at the valet when they returned to the park entrance; there was nothing to gain in longing for the impossible. She was who she was, and the sooner she returned to her own social sphere the better.

*

Mr Richard Critchley was to get one of the biggest surprises he had experienced in the last few months when he visited his friend next. Alexander greeted Richard with a smile and a warm welcome that had not been forthcoming in his dark days.

"Richard! Just the person I needed to speak to! Come in! You've saved me sending round a missive to you," Alexander said, pouring them a drink. He knew Richard did not mind the technique

Alexander used to prevent spillages. A finger inside the glass helped to indicate when the liquid was up to the required level. Not everyone would appreciate such a method, but it meant that the friends could enjoy privacy, and Alexander could still feel like he was master in his own house.

Alexander held out the glass which Richard took, and they both sat down. "So, Alex, what can I do for you? Is it another night out you wish for?" Richard asked pleasantly.

"Never! I'm not that foolish! I need you to find a way that I can speak to Sir Jeremy Basingstoke without needing to go to the house," Alexander explained.

Richard saw the way that Alexander was glowing and immediately became more alert. "Why on earth would you wish to speak to him?"

"I've been working with his dog every morning, and I want to buy him so I can continue the work here in my own home and local area. I think I've found the solution to my confinement."

"You'd better explain," Richard said quietly.

Alexander was only too willing to explain what had gone on and the plans he had for what he hoped Samson would be able to do with further training. "I need to spend far more time with him than I am at the moment," Alexander continued. "An hour each morning, if I'm lucky, just isn't enough."

"Don't you think it will appear odd that you want to buy a dog that has been labelled useless?" Richard asked.

"I don't care about that and neither will Sir Jeremy as long as I pay the right price." Alexander dismissed the worried tone of Richard's voice.

"And won't he think it strange you have so much knowledge of the dog?"

"I did wonder if it would put Miss Basingstoke in an awkward position, but I feel that her uncle will understand," Alexander countered. "I'm willing to give it a try."

"If it doesn't work, the result could be you're leg-shackled to the chit and don't own the dog!"

"Oh ye of little faith," Alexander scoffed, but he could not shake the thought that to be in Miss Basingstoke's company more would be a pleasure indeed, but Richard was being ridiculous; there was no chance that by approaching Sir Jeremy Basingstoke he would end up married. Even if there was a chance, he would have been prepared to take the risk; a fleeting image of him standing at an altar, waiting for Miss Basingstoke to join him flitted through his mind, but in reality marriage to anyone was not an option. "Indulge me in this, Richard. I have to give it a try."

Richard could not refuse to help Alexander, and they sent round a note to Sir Jeremy at his club so that there was less chance of Lady Basingstoke hearing about the scheme before it was finalised. Sir Jeremy joined them as requested and Alexander explained his proposition.

Sir Jeremy sat back after he had listened to the surprising story. He was not an unpleasant man but had been worn weary by many years of living with a controlling woman. "Well, who'd have thought little Amelia would be so considerate to that useless dog," he said softly when being told of Amelia's morning routine.

"You weren't aware of Miss Basingstoke taking the dog for walks?" Richard asked.

"I knew she had done a time or two, but I didn't realise she was doing it every day. None of us is usually below stairs before noon," Sir Jeremy admitted.

"I think she enjoyed the peace of the park before it became busy," Alexander said, struck by the pretty name his companion had. He had never heard her given name used before, and it had not been appropriate for him to ask to use it.

"More like she wanted to rest her ears before Serena came downstairs!" Sir Jeremy said, being brave in a safe environment.

Both gentlemen chose not to respond to the comment for politeness' sake. "I'm presuming that you've no objections to me buying Samson?" Alexander asked.

"Me? No, if you want to buy him, I'd be a fool to refuse! Mind you, you know of his character; I won't be having him back if you change your mind, Captain Worthington. I know you aren't able-bodied but a sale is a sale," Sir Jeremy said, delighted he was getting rid of the animal that had embarrassed him and going to make a profit nonetheless. He had been offered a good price for the dog.

Alexander gave a tight smile. "I won't be returning him."

"Good. That's settled then. Shall we say you'll collect him at four of the clock?" Sir Jeremy offered, keen for the transaction to take place before the Captain could change his mind.

"Are you available to escort me, Richard?" Alexander asked.

"Of course," Richard said easily.

"In that case, I shall bid you gentlemen good day, and I'll see you a little later," Sir Jeremy said, taking his leave.

Richard waited until Sir Jeremy had left the room before speaking to be certain the gentleman was no longer in earshot; he turned to Alexander with a frown on his face. "Are you sure about this Alex?" he asked.

"As sure as I've been about anything," Alexander reassured him.

"And what does Miss Basingstoke think of your scheme?"

Alexander faltered a little. "I haven't discussed it with her," Alexander confessed.

"This afternoon is going to be especially interesting then," Richard said. He wondered about the young woman. She had obviously been going out of doors every morning, every cold and frosty morning no less to meet with Alexander. He was curious about her motives; he had been since that first day they met when he realised she had already been in company with his friend. He could not shake the feeling she had some motive that Alexander did not realise. He thought it would be revealing how events unfolded during the afternoon.

# Chapter 7

Amelia was seated as usual in the drawing room in the late afternoon. Lady Basingstoke and Serena sat close to the fire, bemoaning the draughts that wound their way through the house, but Amelia was not allowed to approach the warmth of the grate. Instead she was confined to the colder side of the room.

Always one for making the best of a situation, Amelia had chosen a seat that was tucked out of the way of the draughts and surrounded herself with cushions which added to her comfort. A thick shawl was hidden under a more delicate looking one; the result being she was snug and especially happy to be out of the direct line of sight of her aunt and cousin. She could listen to their conversation while watching the intermittent snow flurries falling outside the window nearest her. The snow was early this year, and it made her long once more for home. Snow was always more welcome when brothers were around to have snowball fights or sledging expeditions; there would be no such happy frivolities for her while she remained in London.

Amelia was startled when the arrival of Captain Worthington and Mr Critchley was announced by Sir Jeremy as he ushered the two gentleman in the room. All three ladies sat a little straighter, Lady Basingstoke gushing in her welcome, ringing for tea and encouraging the gentlemen to sit close to the fire.

"It's Amelia we've come to speak to," Sir Jeremy explained, indicating that his niece should move closer.

Amelia flushed at the look her aunt and cousin aimed in her direction. "Amelia? What could you possibly want with Amelia?" Lady Basingstoke uttered in genuine bemusement.

"Come, my dear," Sir Jeremy said with a smile at his niece. His confidence had been boosted by his conviction that his wife would be pleased at the amount he was receiving for the dog and the fact that the beast would no longer be resident in the house.

Amelia approached her uncle cautiously. "Yes, Uncle?" she asked.

"I have some good news for you," Sir Jeremy replied with an indulgent smile. "You'll no longer be needed to walk that hound of mine. Captain Worthington here is buying Samson."

Amelia could feel the colour drain from her face at the news. She looked at Mr Critchley and Captain Worthington; Mr Critchley seemed to be watching her closely while Captain Worthington looked distinctively uncomfortable. Amelia looked at her uncle, "I see," she said, her words devoid of feeling.

Sir Jeremy was aware the atmosphere had stilled in the room somewhat and blustered to try and overcome it. "I thought it would be a good idea if you walked around the square with Samson and the Captain before he takes him away." He was trying to cover the fact that he knew they had been meeting each morning. He was sensible enough to know his wife would find a way to punish his niece if she found out the truth.

"I shall fetch my pelisse uncle; I shan't be very long," Amelia said leaving the room. She ran up the stairs, angry with herself that once she was out of sight of everyone tears stung her eyes. She slammed the door of her bedchamber, unconcerned who heard the noise and slumped in a chair. Rubbing her hands over her face, she groaned; what had she expected? From the very beginning she had told herself she should guard her heart, but she obviously had not. Her insides had sunk at the words of her uncle; she had hoped that her captain liked her just a little, but it appeared Samson had been the attraction after all.

Amelia stormed over to her wardrobe and, taking out her pelisse with some force, scattered the other clothes from their hooks. She was still doing it, she fumed to herself. He was not and never would be *her* captain; she was just someone who had been useful to him.

She forced herself to look calmer as she descended the stairs. If her bonnet was pulled onto her curls with a little more force than usual it went unnoticed as she concentrated on pushing the anger and hurt to one side.

Amelia entered the drawing room to a scene that could not help but amuse her despite her other feelings. Serena was standing, also dressed in her outdoor clothes, looking afraid. Samson was seated at the left of Captain Worthington but was growling every time Serena looked at him.

Mr Critchley broke the silence. "Miss Basingstoke has agreed to accompany us for a turn around the square, Miss Amelia, even though it is still snowing slightly."

There was enough information in the tone of Mr Critchley's voice to betray the fact that something had happened while Amelia had been out of the room. She had, in fact, missed some ill-bred words uttered by her cousin when ordered to accompany the party outside by her mother. Lady Basingstoke would never let snow stop her daughter walking out with a handsome gentleman.

"Shall we go?" Amelia asked, and the small party moved forward. Mr Critchley helped Captain Worthington out of the house even though Samson was firmly by his side.

Amelia led the way with Serena muttering in her ear. "I shan't forgive you for this; I could catch my death of cold from being out in this weather!" Serena hissed.

"It has nothing to do with me. I want to be outside as little as you do," Amelia said with a shrug. Her pelisse was made out of thick wool, but she could still feel the cold through it. She had no doubt she was wasting her breath by trying to convince Serena; her cousin took every opportunity to blame her for any inconvenience however irrational her condemnation.

When they had descended the steps to street level, the party rearranged itself with Alexander and Amelia at the front of the group. Before they started to walk Amelia handed the leather strap of Samson's lead to Alexander. "He may have stayed by your side in the park, but I suggest when you are both in the town he is kept on his lead. If he is spooked by anything he would put himself and others in danger. I would hate him to end his days under the wheels of a carriage." Her tone was cool and practical. "We can begin the walk whenever you feel comfortable."

Alexander waited until he heard the voices of Richard and Serena behind him, talking to each other. He did not wish for Serena to overhear anything that would increase Amelia's suffering while she resided in the Basingstoke household. "Miss Basingstoke, I hope you understand my motivation in approaching your uncle," he started, for once hesitant in her company.

"I understand, but I'm surprised it was something that you hadn't mentioned earlier in our acquaintance," came the clipped reply.

Alexander groaned inwardly; Richard had suggested she might get upset, and it was obvious from her cool tone that she was. He had to do something to make her understand; he had too few friends to alienate even one of them. "I'm sorry. I didn't really want to mention it."

"That much is obvious," Amelia said. She stopped walking, and Samson came to a halt. "We have reached the kerbstone at the road edge. Samson needs to learn what to do so that he doesn't walk you into the road and the path of an oncoming equipage."

Richard and Serena soon joined them, being only a few steps behind. After a quick assessment of the situation Richard offered a solution. "Get the dog to sit at every kerb then you can listen for the sounds of hooves before you cross."

Alexander looked unsure. "That's quite a risk; I didn't think of taking such a chance as stepping out into the unknown."

Amelia was still angry with him, but her compassion about his situation was stirred. "Samson is no fool. He wouldn't willingly walk in front of anything that would harm either of you. If you listen but move and Samson hesitates, then trust him; listen more carefully."

"What about when I reach the kerbstone at the other side of the road?" Alexander asked. Cursing that he was showing so much vulnerability before the three others in the party, he was quickly coming to realise he had not thought through the reality of being outside and alone with just the dog for support.

"Let's see what Samson does," Amelia said. "I will be by your side, so I won't let you stumble," she reassured him. The frown

Alexander wore and the concern in his expression was rapidly dissolving her remaining anger. She had been selfish by being angry at him because he had hurt her own vanity; of course, he needed the dog for help. She had known that from the start. Condemning him for her own foolish thoughts was uncharitable, and Amelia inwardly shook herself.

"Even if I deserve it?" Alexander asked quietly.

Amelia chuckled, "Not in front of witnesses. Luckily for you we won't ever be walking alone again. I couldn't give any guarantees of your safety if we were."

Alexander's frown deepened at the thought of not seeing Amelia every morning. He wanted to say something, but needed to concentrate on what he was doing. Yet again, his blindness was getting in the way of his life. Forcing himself to concentrate on the task at hand, he instructed Samson to sit. The group was quiet as Alexander listened carefully until he was happy and then stepped into the road. "Over Samson, over," he said as they walked.

Amelia watched closely as they approached the opposite kerbstone and touched Alexander's arm. "We're nearly at the other side," she said quietly.

Alexander slowed down, but he stepped up onto the pavement without any issue. He smiled with relief as the others followed him. "It was easier than I expected," he explained. "Samson walks slightly ahead of me, so I felt his body rise up when he stepped up for the kerbstone. I must say that it's less nerve-racking stepping up than it is stepping down!"

"Let's continue to walk; we have time to practice on the other roads leading into the square," Amelia said. As a road entered the square at each corner, they would cross a further three if they continued in the direction they were walking before returning to the Basingstoke House.

The group continued on their slow journey, stopping at each kerbstone and waiting while Alexander gave the instruction to sit before listening for the noise of horses and carriages. Amelia did not speak unless it was needed because she could see that Alexander was concentrating on what he was doing and listening intently to the noises of the street. They returned to the stone steps leading up to Basingstoke House, and Serena rubbed her hands.

"I'm glad that excursion is over!" she said with feeling. "It's far too cold to be outside! Would you gentlemen like to take more tea with us?"

"I'd like to repeat what we've just done, if you can bear it," Alexander said. "I'd just like to give Samson another chance to practice what we've been doing."

"Do you not have a square outside your own establishment?" Serena snapped. It was obvious that she no longer perceived Captain Worthington as a good enough catch. Amelia was surprised that she was showing Mr Critchley her true colours though; *he* was still an unmarried gentleman and rich to boot.

Richard thought it prudent to do the gentlemanly thing and assist his friend. "If I could take tea while Worthington walks around the square to his heart's content, that would be lovely Miss Basingstoke. It is too cold to be outside for long today."

Serena seemed pacified and led the way into the house, leaving Amelia and Alexander on the pavement. "Shall we?" Alexander asked.

"Lead on," Amelia replied, rubbing her hands slightly; even with the protection of gloves they were a little cold, but she could not complain if another turn around the square would increase Alexander's confidence.

They walked in silence until the first road was crossed successfully. Then Alexander relaxed enough to open the conversation. "I am sorry I'm taking your ally away from you," he said quietly. Serena's behaviour had been impolite enough to give him a glimpse into how difficult life must be for Amelia.

"I will be saddened to lose him, but you need him more than I do. With you he'll be well cared for. When I return home goodness knows what would happen to him," Amelia replied, fair as always.

"You're going home?" Alexander asked sharply. When in her company he could forget she was only a temporary visitor, but her words had jolted the reality of her situation to the forefront of his mind.

"I think three seasons as a wallflower are enough for anyone!" Amelia said, her tone was jovial, but she was disappointed. She had hoped for more, to be married and settled. Returning home at three and twenty, which she would be at the end of the season, would guarantee her confirmation as an old maid.

"I'll be sorry to see you go," Alexander said honestly.

"You didn't know me prior to these last four weeks; I'm convinced you shall cope admirably without me once I have returned to Charmouth." Her own feelings she could not be so flippant about.

"You live in Charmouth?" Alexander asked. "I have a number of friends who live in Lyme."

"I'm not surprised; virtually everyone in Lyme has some connection to the sea," Amelia replied.

"It's a pretty place."

"It is, but I don't venture there much. I tend to stay in Charmouth unless my father has business in Lyme. Then I do take the opportunity to accompany him. There are a wider range of shops in Lyme, and I am frivolous enough to enjoy spending my pennies in them."

Alexander was once again reminded how different their lives were. Of course the family would not be constantly visiting Lyme; without doubt every farthing had to be used wisely. Trips to the next town incurred a cost. Only people like him, who had made his fortune because of the chances his heritage offered him, could waste money by visiting friends on a whim.

They completed the square, and Amelia came to a standstill at her uncle's home. "I think Samson is fully aware of what is expected of him now."

"He learns so quickly, it's astounding," Alexander said, ruffling the neck of the dog, who had sat on the pavement once his new master came to a halt.

"He's a very intelligent dog," Amelia said in agreement. "From what Uncle Jeremy has said, his breed is very easy to train; I suppose sometimes there is such a thing as too intelligent, though. He just didn't want to chase birds, either alive or dead, and I can't really blame him," Amelia said with a smile, looking fondly at the dog. She was convinced he would be happy with Alexander; it was clear the dog was already dedicated to him.

The butler came to the door, and Amelia asked if Alexander would like to enter for tea. Alexander refused. "If you don't mind I would like to keep Samson by my side and return home."

"Would you please ask Mr Critchley if he is ready to depart, Wilson?" Amelia asked the butler who nodded and disappeared inside the house.

Alexander reached out his hand, and Amelia placed hers in it. "Miss Basingstoke, I owe you such a great debt."

"Samson has done the work," Amelia said, ever dismissive of a compliment.

"I owe you the debt from even before I'd met Samson," Alexander clarified. "On that first night, you seemed to shine a light into my very dark world. I can never thank you enough for talking to me even though I was in the worst of moods."

"I'm glad I helped; you cheered my evening as well," Amelia admitted.

"I wish I could secure a dance with you one day," Alexander said quietly.

"If you could, we would not be having this conversation. We are from different worlds, Captain Worthington, but I am glad you have Samson. Please look after him." It was the first time Amelia had voiced what they had both thought over the weeks they had known each other. It was the only way Amelia could keep the reality of their friendship at the forefront of her mind; to do otherwise would be to mourn what had never been hers.

"Our paths are never going to cross again are they?" Alexander said, the realisation of losing her hitting him fully for the first time. He felt a lump of lead form in his stomach and somehow knew instinctively it would not be easy to remove.

"No," came the quiet response.

Alexander kissed Amelia's hand. It was inappropriate, but convention be damned! He was losing the one person who had gone out of her way to help him these last few weeks, and now his actions had ultimately been the cause of their separation. He heard Amelia's intake of breath but, before he could say more, Richard came quickly down the steps.

"Worthington?" Richard asked quietly. He noticed Amelia's distraught expression and suddenly had the feeling she was not the shallow, calculating miss he had first suspected. She had true feelings for his friend, and she was hurting. He was gentleman enough to have sympathy with the young woman even though no one could offer her hope.

"It's time to go home," Alexander said turning to Richard. "Miss Basingstoke, I wish you every health and happiness for your future."

"Thank you," Amelia replied with a curtsey and, with bows, the two gentlemen turned away from her. She walked into the house and, instead of being able to grieve the loss she felt, she was greeted by Serena.

"You were throwing yourself at a blind man who thankfully couldn't see what an exhibition you were making of yourself! How desperate are you? Just wait until mother hears about this!" Serena said gleefully.

"Oh, Serena, go and find another impoverished relative to torment because they are in no position to fight back! I've had enough of you and your bitterness!" Amelia snapped. She left her cousin standing in the hall in shock at the anger aimed at her. Amelia knocked on her uncle's study door. It was time to go home.

Chapter 8

London early December 1806

Amelia sat on the benches at the ball without the usual feelings of disappointment that the time spent sitting at the edges of society could cause. Tonight was her last night in London, and she would never enter the confines of the City again; of that she was quite sure. She had managed to persuade her uncle to let her return home only by telling him she would leave his protection and make her way under her own volition if he did not agree to her scheme of returning to her family.

Sir Jeremy had submitted to a forceful character as he always did, but he insisted on her staying for a week longer, enabling him to accompany her to Charmouth himself. He had some business to attend to within a mile or two of his brother's house, and he was willing to accompany Amelia home. It had been a compromise that Amelia could agree to; one week in her aunt and cousin's company seemed like nothing when reflecting over the previous two and a half years she had spent with them.

Her aunt had graciously allowed her to attend this last ball. Amelia was sure it was so that she could point out the unmarriageable one of the family, lamenting what a trial it had been for her to deal with, failing to mention all the work Amelia had done when her aunt could not stir herself, which was more often than not. Amelia reflected that, if nothing else, she had become a better seamstress on this trip.

Amelia sat, her foot tapping to the music, watching the couples dancing the cotillion. She saw Mr Critchley amongst the crowd of people long before he reached her. He was a finely dressed young man, his frock coat made of the finest wool and the satin of his waistcoat a striking contrast against the thicker material. His breeches clung to his legs, and his boots shone in the candlelight. He was rightly one of the most admired men in any ballroom, but to Amelia he just did not have the presence of Captain Worthington. It was clear Richard was making his way towards her, and he smiled at her when their eyes met. She was surprised at his approach; he had previously been wary of being around her family for which, though a pity for he was an entertaining character, she did not think any less of him.

"Miss Basingstoke, I hope you are well," Richard bowed before Amelia.

"I am, thank you, Mr Critchley," Amelia replied with a smile.

"I've come to ask for your hand for the next two if you are willing and not already taken?"

"As you see I'm fighting off hordes of admirers, but I shall make myself available for you," Amelia said with a falsely coy look.

"I'm honoured," Richard grinned, appreciating the unaffected response. "In the meantime, may I join you?"

"Of course." Amelia shuffled along the bench to make room.

"I've been spending quite a lot of time with that animal," Richard said, flicking out the tails of his exquisitely made deep red frock coat before making himself comfortable on the bench.

"Captain Worthington?" Amelia said with a mischievous look.

Richard chuckled. "Oh, Miss Basingstoke, you should know never to give friends the ammunition to torment the other. I shall have fun with that comment!"

Amelia smiled, "I would expect nothing less, but tell me about Samson. Has he settled into his new home?"

"Yes, and it seems the days of being disobedient are long past. I doubt your uncle would recognise him now. Worthington has him working so much he is as docile as can be. It's not all work though; he is taken to Green Park every morning and evening for a run off lead," Richard explained.

"Yes, working did seem to tire him as much as a good run did," Amelia agreed. "I'm glad he's settled in well; I thought he would but there was always a little doubt."

"Yes, I half expected to find Worthington abandoned in the street one day, but it appears the dog takes his responsibilities seriously."

"It must give Captain Worthington a much needed sense of freedom."

"It does."

"I can't imagine any of my brothers coping with being so reliant on others."

The dance finished, and Richard stood and offered his hand to Amelia. "Shall we take our place?" he asked leading her through the crowds to reach the dancefloor.

Richard was an amenable partner, and Amelia was kept entertained throughout their two dances. It was a nice end to her stay, experiencing the pleasure of dancing with a handsome man; that he would never match the appeal of another Amelia refused to let herself dwell on; it would take away the shine of the current dance.

After the two dances ended Richard escorted Amelia to the edge of the ballroom. She was grateful he did not return her to the benches, enabling her to pretend she was equal to all the other young ladies milling about the room.

"I hope we will see you one morning in Green Park," Richard said, not needing to explain who the 'we' was. "I can't say I go every morning, but Worthington does."

Amelia's smile was tinged with sadness. "I'm afraid that is a pleasure I shall not be able to join in. I'm returning home tomorrow."

"But the season hasn't finished!" Richard said in genuine surprise. He had some idea of Amelia's feelings and was surprised that she was willingly removing herself from any chance of seeing Alexander.

"I know," Amelia replied, stopping herself from uttering words that would sound bitter. There was no point in longing for something that was not meant to be. "It's time I returned home to my family; I have a longing to be with them for Christmas. I've not seen them for more than two years."

"That is a shame."

"We should be close to the ones we love at this time of year. I have had two Christmas's away from home; I don't want to experience a third," Amelia said quietly.

Richard smiled and bowed to Amelia. "Forgive me for saying but I admit to being wary of your motives when we first met Miss Basingstoke, but that was my poor judgement. It has been a pleasure to meet you."

"I'm aware the name of Basingstoke inspires fear in most single men," Amelia replied drily.

Richard laughed. "I wish you a speedy, safe journey." He bowed and left Amelia smiling at his retreating form.

*

Alexander was struggling. He was working Samson for a large part of each day. Peterson and Richard had been on hand to help with the practice sessions as Samson was taught each action he was being asked to do. Then they would follow Alexander as he worked with Samson to retrace a route somewhere just to make sure the dog was happy and confident.

Each morning and evening Alexander took Samson to Green Park with his footman and let the dog have a run without being restricted by Alexander's presence. The work was paying off; only two weeks had passed since Samson had moved in and already Alexander visited a coffee shop every morning to pass the time of day with its other occupants.

The novelty of seeing a dog leading a person had encouraged some of the gentlemen to approach Alexander and start a conversation while he drank coffee. Once the initial approach had been made everyone, including Alexander, had relaxed somewhat, which enabled more natural conversations to develop. Now, each morning he would be hailed by someone who would be willing to tell him of the latest news from the racing or shooting world. It seemed their initial view of him as too limited to add anything useful to a conversation was no longer the case. Alexander wondered if it had more to do with his inability to be as pleasant as he should have been and their nervousness about such a unique situation.

Alexander had also approached, with Richard's support, his favourite club, White's. They had enquired as to whether Samson would be welcome within its walls. An agreement was made on condition that the dog behaved itself, so each afternoon Alexander walked to 37 St James' Street to partake of refreshment and more male company. He chose to stay with one club; Samson knew exactly where to go once the instruction of 'Take me to the club, Samson,' was given. Alexander was aware that he did not wish to overload the animal, and White's was easily accessible from Alexander's own house on Jermyn Street.

So, for the first time since the battle of Trafalgar Alexander was socialising more than he had done since his return. He realised he would never fully rejoin society; there would be no more ballrooms for him, but he felt a freedom that, a few months ago, he never thought he would have.

He should be happy he acknowledged to himself. He *was* happy, but there was a problem. There was something missing. He raised the subject with Richard one afternoon while his sat in one of White's comfortable leather chairs, Samson lying contentedly at Alexander's feet.

"I go to Green Park every morning," Alexander started.

"I know; Peterson has told me it doesn't matter how cold the night has been, you always venture outdoors," Richard said. A closer relationship had developed between the two friends and the valet. It was unusual for such an instance to occur, but they were dealing with a unique situation, and it required more communication than was normal.

"I'd have thought Miss Basingstoke would have wished to see how Samson was faring," Alexander said, wishing he could see the expression on his friend's face at the mention of the young lady.

One of the main disadvantages with blindness was being unable to read what the person you were communicating with was thinking. The voice did not always betray what thoughts or emotions were being felt the way an expression did.

Richard paused before speaking. Alexander had flushed slightly when mentioning the young lady's name, something Richard had never seen happen before. Alexander's voice also betrayed longing. "So it wasn't just the dog that attracted you to the park each morning before you purchased him?"

"No," Alexander replied honestly. He remembered clearly that Richard had dismissed Amelia as 'not his type' when he had first met her and did not know if he would ridicule Alexander now, but it was a risk he had to take. There was no other way of receiving news of a young woman whom he longed to be near.

"I see," Richard said trying to decide what to tell his friend.

Alexander decided to be open with Richard. "She was the only person apart from yourself who treated me like a normal human being. I never thought after the ball that I would ever meet her again, but then she burst into my life that morning in the park. I tried to concentrate on the dog; I think I was doing it at first, but I realise now that it was also the times we talked that I looked forward to."

"She isn't like her relations," Richard admitted.

"No! Not at all. In fact they've made her life hell, which was another reason I hoped she would still walk in Green Park every morning. I know she used Samson as a reason for escape."

"Alex, she's no longer in London," Richard said.

"What? Why? What's happened?" Alexander said, so forcefully that Samson jumped up, immediately aware that something was wrong.

"I saw her at Lindhurst's ball last week. I actually had two dances with her; she was a delightful dance partner, very light on her feet."

"Get to the point," Alexander ground out, insanely jealous that Richard had had the opportunity of dancing with Amelia. He wanted the chance to hold her as they moved, but he never would, even if she were to stay in London for the next ten years.

"Her uncle was taking her home soon after the ball. I can't quite remember whether it was the next day or a few days afterwards, but she was definitely going home."

"But it's the middle of the season!" Alexander said, trying to grasp onto something that would prevent her from leaving even though he knew the season would not keep Amelia in London.

"I think she'd had enough," Richard replied confirming what Alexander knew to be true.

"Damn it!" Alexander cursed.

Richard watched his friend. Alexander might not be able to read a person's expression, but he could still betray his feelings through expressions. "I didn't realise you felt so strongly about her," Richard finally said quietly.

Alexander slumped back in his seat. "Who am I trying to fool Richard?" He asked, a bereft expression on his face. Samson sensed that his master was upset and put his nose under Alexander's hand in reassurance. Alexander stroked the dog absentmindedly. "I've just realised how much I need to meet with her again."

"What do you want to achieve?" Richard had concerns that he would not want Amelia if he had seen her; she was not stunningly beautiful and the old Alexander had had very high standards in regards to beauty. For once it did not seem fair to the young lady if she was only wanted because there was no one else.

"I don't know! Oh damn my eyes! Richard, I need to visit her; will you help me?" Alexander appealed to his friend. His feelings were completely mixed up; he had no idea what he wanted to say to Amelia, but the thought of never speaking to her again, never being in her company again, terrified him like a whole sea full of French ships had not.

"I'll do as you wish," Richard promised, but he was not convinced that Alexander would feel so strongly about the chit if he had sight. He smiled to himself; only a few weeks ago he had been wary of Amelia; now he was concerned about his friend's motivation. It would be poor of Alexander to raise the hopes of the girl. The complexities of relationships were enough to put a man off marriage forever.

*

Alexander had returned home and was ensconced in his study with Samson at his feet when the door opened and in walked his brother.

"I said I'd announce myself," Anthony said crossing the room to greet his younger brother. "What's this I've been hearing from the staff that you are out every day without an escort?"

"Hello, Anthony," Alexander said, standing in greeting and being wrapped in an embrace that only Anthony could give. "I never go out without an escort. Meet my trusty steed, Samson."

Samson was already standing; the moment Alexander stood, Samson sprang into action, ready for any command that would be given. Anthony looked at the dog. "He's a good-looking animal. I'm not sure that I could put my trust in him if I were blind."

"It takes some getting used to," Alexander agreed, moving to the drinks cabinet to pour his brother a drink. "Once he's learned a new route, we both soon gain a lot of confidence."

"I'm glad," Anthony responded. Already he could see a marked difference since the last time he had seen his brother. He was moving with confidence but, more than that, he was holding himself as he used to—upright like a man sure of himself not the hunched shell of a person he had become.

"I can't explain the feeling of freedom in simply being outside without needing to be attached to another person. If I hadn't found Samson, I sincerely believe I would have gone mad," Alexander said with feeling. "Now, what brings you to London?"

"You, of course," Anthony replied. "I know there's lots of entertainments to keep you in the City, but I wondered if you would like to join the family for Christmas?" Anthony had married a woman who liked the London social scene as little as he did, so they both avoided it as much as possible. If he had to travel because of business, very often he would stay with Alexander for the least amount of time needed to complete his business and then return to the countryside and his family.

Alexander took a sip of his brandy; a frown had emerged at Anthony's words. "I won't be joining you this Christmas."

"Oh, come on! I know we can't compete with the invitations that will be piling on your desk, but we have got some entertainments planned!"

Alexander smiled a bitter smile. "My desk is bereft of invitations today and every day."

"How so?" Anthony said genuinely puzzled. His brother had always been extremely popular.

"Our society prefers its members to be perfect," Alexander replied.

"That's ridiculous!" Anthony exploded.

Alexander shrugged, no longer looking bitter. "I won't lie and say it hasn't been a hell of a few months, but do you know something? I'm glad I found out what my so-called friends are really like. If you'll excuse the pun, I've had my eyes opened these last few months about what is important and what isn't."

"I never thought I'd hear those words from you," Anthony acknowledged, watching his brother carefully. It seemed that the changes had gone beyond the physical.

"Was I that arrogant?" Alexander asked, raising an eyebrow.

"Let's just say you fitted in with your friends perfectly," Anthony replied truthfully.

Alexander laughed. "All stiff-upper-lipped and glowering? I was told that was the impression I gave when I let Richard take me to a ballroom. It's a mistake I won't be making again, but I'm glad I went."

Anthony had heard about the fiasco and was surprised at Alexander's response to it. He was so used to the angry brother that had emerged after the accident that this new person sitting before him was taking some time to get used to. "I'm afraid to ask why," Anthony said good-naturedly.

"I had the good fortune of meeting someone there who has been a true friend to me over these last weeks, as well as Richard of course."

"A lady?"

"Yes."

"Who is she?" Anthony was immediately interested.

"Oh, no one any of us knew before. She was definitely beneath our notice because of our self-imposed importance. She is a Miss without dowry; in fact, firmly on the shelf," Alexander said being honest with his brother.

Anthony was cautious but still interested. "And she is now a good friend. I would like to make her acquaintance before I return home."

"She's gone."

"Gone? Where?"

"To Charmouth, and that's the reason I won't be spending Christmas with you," Alexander said firmly.

"Is that wise?" Anthony asked.

"Probably not, particularly as I've no idea what to do when I get there," Alexander admitted.

"Alex, I've seen you hide from your struggles, and now you are facing them with what appears to be great results. I would hate to see you have a further set-back," Anthony said gently.

"Does it make sense if I say that if I don't hear her voice at least for one more time I will regret it for the rest of my life?" Alexander said, finally admitting some of the turmoil he had felt since there had been no morning meetings with Amelia.

"In that case I wish you a good journey and hope that some guardian angel is looking down on you kindly. I want you to be happy, Alex."

"So do I, Anthony. So do I," Alexander replied, a little overwhelmed at the feelings that were caused by the thought of being in Amelia's company once more.

# Chapter 9

Alexander was not the only one missing the contact they had enjoyed through their brief acquaintance. Amelia was distinctly out of sorts since she had returned home. Oh, it was wonderful to see her mother and father again and to be welcomed back with open arms into a family that loved and appreciated her, but she was not completely happy, and she did not know what to do about it.

A week after her return, Amelia had secreted herself in the small room that was used as a study and library. It was the room she had used the most since arriving home; it effectively provided peace and a place to hide. Their house was not large enough to provide many places one could separate oneself from the other members of the family but, for the first time in her life, Amelia felt as if she needed that escape.

Two window seats provided comfort and a place to read and think without going outside, probably the only other place one could find solace in a home that housed a large family when everyone was in residence. The large desk dominated the small room, allowing only the chair behind the desk and two smaller chairs near the fireplace. A side table completed the furniture for the room with everything that was needed and no unnecessary extravagance. Shelves filled the one wall that had no window, door or fireplace. There were books, but the shelves held more space than actual books; when money was scarce, books were an unnecessary luxury.

Mr Basingstoke walked into the room, noticing his daughter seated in the corner on the window seat. She looked small, curled up in an effort to be comfortable and warm. Mr Basingstoke frowned as he watched his daughter gazing at a book she held, obviously not reading, but deep in thought. It was time that father and daughter spoke candidly; he had observed her on a number of occasions since her return and was concerned about his child.

"My dear, why aren't you walking to the vicarage with your Mama?" he asked, sitting on the window seat so Amelia had to shuffle her knees further under her chin to allow him access.

Mr Basingstoke's hair had gone white very early, making him look older than he actually was, although some wondered whether it was the effect of having eight riotous boys to bring up. He had a calming and loving nature without being oppressive; all his children adored him. He was in contrast to a mother who had become, as she aged, more concerned with what could go wrong in life than with being thankful for what she had. Mr Basingstoke still loved her dearly.

Mr Basingstoke clothes might not have been the fine quality of his brother; on close examination his shirts would show signs of wear that would never be accepted in Sir Jeremy's wardrobe, but Mr Basingstoke had the peace and contentment his brother lacked in his home life. Mr Basingstoke had eight sons of whom he was immensely proud and a daughter who was the apple of his eye. They had been very close before she left for the delights of London, but now he was treading carefully to find out exactly what was amiss.

"I couldn't face going today. I asked to be excused; Mama was happy to go alone," Amelia replied.

"You've appeared out of sorts since your return Amelia. It is good to have you home, but I had hoped you would make a good match in London. I had resigned myself to losing you to some beau or other," Mr Basingstoke said fondly.

Amelia smiled at her father. "It appears you shall have me around forever. I hope you don't mind the extra burden."

"Mind? You'll never be considered a burden, but it's natural for a parent to want to see his child happy." There was a slight pause. "You aren't happy at the moment, my dear."

Amelia blinked quickly; of course her father would notice something was amiss; he, above anyone else in the family, was in tune with how she functioned. "I'm happy to be home. London didn't suit me. In addition, my aunt and Serena, well, we have completely different characters," she said honestly, while trying to be diplomatic in her response.

"But? Was there no one that made your heart race a little?" Mr Basingstoke prompted patiently.

"There was a gentleman," Amelia confessed. She took a breath, glad to be able to speak about Alexander to someone who would understand in some way. "Does it make sense if I say that from the moment I first set eyes on him, I knew he was more perfect to me than anyone else I'd met or would ever meet?"

"Go on," Mr Basingstoke encouraged, glad that Amelia was finally confiding in him. Her withdrawn demeanour since her arrival had been a worry.

"I saw him at the start of my first season. He was so tall and strong; he seemed to fill every ballroom or party he attended. The moment he walked in the room, I knew where he was." Amelia thought back to those first few times she had seen Captain Worthington. He had filled the room; it was as if every other man shrank when they were near him; none could compare. He had looked magnificent in his blue uniform with the gold braiding reflecting off the many candles. His hair had always been tied in a queue; no foppish curls for him. His laugh had rumbled through Amelia as if it were a physical thing. When he danced, he chatted and laughed, obviously flirting with whichever lucky partner he had chosen; but he had never seemed to take anything seriously, teasing so much he would have his companion constantly blushing. Amelia had watched, drawn to him, longing to be the one who made him laugh but being realistic about her situation.

"And did he return your feelings?"

"No!" Amelia laughed. "He didn't even know I existed. We were never introduced; we never even danced in the same set." She chose to leave out that she actually danced very little; there was nothing to be gained by distressing her father when he had expressed such high hopes for her trip. "He was so much better than me, a Captain of his majesty's navy and a very good one by all accounts."

"I don't like to hear you saying that someone is better than you," Mr Basingstoke chided. "We are all put on this earth as equals."

"You know that isn't true Papa, and it's never as obvious as when one is attending an entertainment where the *ton* is present. They make sure that anyone who is beneath their notice knows their place."

"And he was one of those, I'm presuming. I cannot see the attraction at the moment."

"You were not a girl of twenty, Papa!" Amelia smiled. "He left last year to join Nelson and was hailed a hero, but he was injured badly, and no one saw him for over a year."

"And then?"

"He returned to Society in November. He's blind Papa, and they all avoided him! He was their hero but, because he was no longer perfect, he was ignored!" Amelia did not try to hide the disgust she felt against everyone who had used Alexander ill.

"So, he was introduced to you then?" Mr Basingstoke asked, trying to read between the lines of the story. It was clear that Amelia had feelings about the Captain, but he wanted to find out exactly what had happened.

"In a manner of speaking. The first time we met, he had been placed next to me on the benches where the wallflowers sit. He was not impressed," she replied with a smile. "But then we met by accident when I was exercising Uncle Jeremy's dog; I wrote to you about him."

"Ah, yes, the infamous Samson."

"Samson astounded us all by turning into the perfect animal whenever he was near Captain Worthington. He is the captain's eyes. We used to train Samson and, I suppose Captain Worthington to some extent, every morning in Green Park."

The way Amelia's eyes had lit up had not gone unnoticed; neither had the flush on her cheeks. "I hope he behaved like a gentleman," Mr Basingstoke said quietly.

"He did Papa; he was more interested in the dog than in me. I could have been anyone; it was Samson who was important," Amelia responded dejectedly.

"So, he spoke to you when you were useful."

"Yes. No. Oh, it wasn't as bad as that! We did talk, but he would never want the likes of me."

"Would you like to expand on that condemning description of yourself before I shake you for being a buffoon?" Mr Basingstoke rarely lost his temper, but he sounded exasperated at his daughter's self-depreciation.

Amelia laughed. "I'm being realistic! Our lives are too different; I had been a romantic fool and allowed my thoughts to run away with themselves. He did nothing wrong."

"I'm not sure I agree with you on that point, but I hope, when you do marry, it will be to someone who values you fully," Mr Basingstoke said with feeling.

"I'm nearly three and twenty, Papa. I'm firmly on the shelf." Amelia was not looking for pity; she was being pragmatic.

"And yet you returned early. There are still months of the season left."

"Christmas is not special when away from one's family. I've missed you all, and there was no one dancing with me, let alone paying their addresses. I would rather be with my family."

Mr Basingstoke felt saddened that his only daughter— the light of his life—had not enjoyed what he had hoped would be the making of her. He admitted parental bias, but she was a handsome girl who had wit and intelligence to add to her attractiveness. He came to the conclusion the London gentlemen had let a diamond slip through their fingers. What he thought of Captain Worthington was even more censorious. Mr Basingstoke was convinced that he had used Amelia, knowing full well she was smitten with him. That thought would keep his lips in a grim line for the rest of the day.

"You will get your wish for a family Christmas this year," Mr Basingstoke said, changing the subject to a more pleasant one. He now knew what was ailing his daughter and had hopes that, after a Christmas with her whole family, she would rally once more.

"Are all the boys going to be home?" Amelia asked, excited at the thought of seeing her brothers again. She could visit the two brothers who had their own farms; they lived within a few miles of home, but the others were further away.

"Yes, I've received a letter from William; his ship has docked, and he is making his way home as we speak."

"Oh, wonderful! I can't wait to see him."

"Bernard and John will only be with us for Christmas Day, neither will leave their farms for any longer, but the boys are arriving from school tomorrow, and Harold and George will be here the day before Christmas Eve."

"What about Peter?" Amelia asked. The brother who was taking Orders had not been mentioned.

"Oh, he's already here; he arrived about an hour ago," Mr Basingstoke said with a smile as Amelia jumped from her seat, all malady gone and ran from the room in search of her brother.

*

Snow was to be the biggest problem for the family gathering. The night of Peter's arrival saw a large snow fall. Amelia stood before the morning room window almost blinded by the brightness of the scene before her. The ground was covered in a good six inches of snow. Every bough and branch was coated in its new white blanket. Some of the smaller bushes looked weighed down with their unexpected heavy load. Few carriages would brave the journey today in fear of driving off the road.

"I hope Benjamin and Thomas make it," Amelia said for the tenth time as she stood looking out of the drawing room window. Her fingers traced the incrustation of ice that had formed on the insides of the glass as she stood look-out for her brothers.

"I'd enjoy the peace while you can," Peter teased, enjoying the warmth the large fire was producing.

"Absence makes you forget everyone's faults. All my brothers became almost angelic in my mind while I was away," Amelia said with a smile.

"Ha! I think some halos will have slipped by the end of the day!" Peter smirked, knowing full well what mischief his two youngest brothers would cause with so much snow at their disposal.

Amelia and Peter were soon joined by their mother and father. No one was prepared to move far from the warmth of the fire on a day that did not tempt one outside; all of them gathering together in only a few rooms reduced the need to have fires in every grate.

"I hope Benjamin and Thomas don't try to reach home today. They should lodge in an inn until the snow melts a little," Mrs Basingstoke fussed, wrapping the thickest shawl she owned close around her shoulders. She had not gone grey early as her husband had, but she had worried herself into an older looking face than she should have, frown lines carving deep groves in her forehead.

"They're young and strong; they'll be fine. If the roads are blocked, they are more than able to walk a few miles," their older brother defended them.

"They're here!" Amelia said excitedly, spotting two figures appearing on the lane, but then she paused and flushed a deep red. "I was mistaken; it isn't them."

"Surely no one is visiting today?" Mrs Basingstoke asked in disbelief. Never one to stir outside if the ground was wet, she could not imagine anyone being foolish enough to stir out of doors in six inches of snow.

"Amelia?" Mr Basingstoke asked quietly having a sudden suspicion as to why his daughter looked perturbed.

Amelia looked at her father, panic in her eyes. She had no idea what the visit meant, but it could not be passed off as something of a coincidence. Moments passed where the father and daughter communicated without words. One gently questioning while the other conveyed surprise and, to her shame, hope. Peter had moved to the window but, not knowing the reason for Amelia's sudden flush, watched the two figures approach with an understandable, but not excessive, amount of curiosity. A knock at the door prevented Amelia from being forced to try and explain who was visiting, but it was clear her father had guessed at least one of the party about to be announced.

The housekeeper entered the room. "Mr Critchley and Captain Worthington are here to pay their respects to Miss Amelia, Sir," she addressed Mr Basingstoke.

"Show them in and please arrange for something warm to drink to be served. I'm sure both would appreciate something hot after walking through the snow," Mr Basingstoke directed, before standing in front of the fireplace in readiness to welcome his unexpected guests.

Richard led Alexander into the drawing room. Mr Basingstoke crossed the room before anything was said. "Gentlemen, welcome to our home on this dreadful morning. At least the sun is out for a while. I'm Amelia's father and this is my wife and one of my sons, Peter."

Richard shook Mr Basingstoke's hand and bowed to his wife. With a look to Peter he expressed the need for Peter to approach them, which he did.

Alexander held out his hand and shook Peter's hand when the young man placed his in Alexander's. "Are you the seafaring brother?" Alexander asked with a smile.

"No, that's my brother William. He's not home at present, although we are expecting him before Christmas," Peter replied easily. "I'm the one taking Orders."

"Ah yes, I remember," Alexander said, relaying to all the party that he had conversed beyond the inane social pleasantries with their relative.

Amelia was the last to approach the pair; her stomach was fluttering so much she was afraid her internal butterflies were in danger of exploding out of her. "Mr Critchley, Captain Worthington. How are you?" she curtsied.

The gentlemen bowed and responded that they were both well.

"You have ventured out without Samson?" Amelia asked Alexander.

"I told you she'd be more interested in the dog than you," Richard said to Alexander, making Amelia flush deep red. It was harder to remain unfazed when being teased with some of your family looking on; especially when one of those family members had been a confidante just the day before.

Amelia was embarrassed, but her natural humour came to the fore. "I'd always say the dog won, even if it was just to annoy."

"You've spent too much time with Richard," Alexander harrumphed.

Mrs Basingstoke invited the gentlemen to be seated, and all watched with interest as Richard guided his friend to the nearest seat. The housekeeper brought a tray of tea and edibles and, as Mrs Basingstoke poured tea and filled plates with cake and biscuits, Mr Basingstoke was able to watch his daughter.

Amelia had taken the cup and saucer from her mother and approached Alexander. She touched his hand with the saucer and waited until he had taken the drink from her. She then touched her hand to his empty hand and, when Alexander had rested his hand on hers, she moved it to a little side table.

"You can put your cup on this table if you wish," she said quietly.

"Thank you," Alexander responded. He would always be at a disadvantage in a strange situation but, with unobtrusive help, he was able to feel more comfortable. Amelia then handed Alexander a plate of biscuits and described what was on the plate. "It sounds delicious," Alexander smiled at her.

"You're a long way from London gentlemen. Do you have family nearby?" Mr Basingstoke asked when everyone was settled and eating.

"I have friends in Lyme. We are staying with them for a few days in Upper Lyme," Alexander said.

"It is a trek to reach Charmouth from Upper Lyme!" Mrs Basingstoke said in surprise. "And in such conditions."

"I owe Miss Basingstoke a debt for introducing me to Samson; I could not visit Lyme and not pay my respects," Alexander said easily.

"But in this weather!" Mrs Basingstoke insisted.

"I don't mind the snow. It is difficult to walk in especially when being led, I admit, but I found it provides an unseen advantage."

"What's that?" Amelia asked before her mother could say anything more about how inappropriate their visit was.

"I normally only see darkness. Shadows and differing shades of grey and black. But the snow is so bright that, for the first time since the accident, I've seen light. I wouldn't go as far as saying that I've seen white, but it's definitely been brighter," Alexander explained to the company.

"It must have been really hard for you," Peter said. "William told us about you on his last visit home. You were a hero on the day."

"I've never felt like one," Alexander admitted. "I was trying to get my men and the ship out intact. I managed to do it, just."

"A difficult battle," Mr Basingstoke acknowledged.

"It was, but we out fought the French in a number of ways. Reflecting on the battle afterwards, it felt as if everything was in our favour."

"I will always thank God our son returned uninjured," Mrs Basingstoke said with a shudder.

They were interrupted by a knocking on the door. The rat-tat-tat inflicted made it obvious, to the family, at least who was knocking at the door.

"Please excuse us a moment; it appears the snow has not hindered our two youngest boys in returning home," Mr Basingstoke said good-humouredly.

"We should leave," Richard said making to move.

"Not at all!" Mr Basingstoke responded. "Amelia, stay with our guests whilst we sort out the boys. I can only imagine what state they will be in."

The room fell silent as all the Basingstokes left the room except Amelia. Richard decided to help the conversation along. "So, are you missing London, Miss Basingstoke?"

"Not at all!" Amelia replied with a laugh. "I hope never to have the need to visit again. I certainly had my fill of the frivolities."

"The benches will never be the same again," Alexander said with mock sorrow.

"Who are you visiting?" Amelia asked, changing the subject, curious to know if they shared the same acquaintance.

"A retired Admiral I served under as a young officer. I learned a lot from him and always intended visiting him."

"So you are to be away from your families at Christmas?" Amelia asked.

"No, it's a short visit," Richard responded.

"Oh," Amelia was suddenly disappointed their visit would not be longer. "It's a shame I wasn't able to see Samson before you left."

"If the snow isn't so bad, we can bring him for a visit tomorrow before we leave Lyme," Alexander offered. He did not need to have sight to know the expression on Richard's face at his words. Throughout the trip, Richard had been expressing his feelings on travelling at this time of year and in the weather that had descended on them. Alexander without doubt would have to withstand a lecture from his friend as soon as they left the house.

"I would like that very much, thank you," Amelia responded.

"It is time we returned to the Admiral's House, Alex," Richard said, standing. "Miss Basingstoke has two brothers to welcome home."

"We are all to be together this Christmas; it's wonderful to be home with everyone," Amelia said happily.

"No cousins?" Alexander teased.

"Definitely no cousins!" Amelia laughed. She led the gentlemen out of the drawing room and made her curtsey in the hallway. Richard made his bow but Alexander held out his hand. Amelia placed hers in his; it was good to feel how her hand felt small in his large one as he raised her hand to his lips and kissed it.

"I'm blaming sight loss for forward behaviour," Alexander said with a grin at Amelia. "Until tomorrow, Miss Basingstoke."

"Good-bye," Amelia whispered continuing to feel the burn of his lips on her bare skin long after the gentlemen had left the house.

# Chapter 10

Amelia tried not to stand at the windows watching for Richard and Alexander; she really did, but the morning seemed to be dragging and, although it had rained overnight, the snow would still restrict easy movement as it was now a deep covering of slush. Her three brothers had ventured out doors to choose a suitable Yule Log and gather holly to decorate the house; it was tradition for every picture frame and windowsill to be filled with evergreens the children collected each year. Amelia had declined the invitation to accompany them, an unknown action previously. Although from experience, she would have been covered in snow and extremely wet if past years were anything to go by when accompanying brothers who enjoyed targeting each other with snowballs.

Amelia had lain awake long into the night reflecting on the unexpected visit. Oh, how good it had been to see him again! She had known she missed Alexander, but the way her heart lifted as he walked into the morning room, she would never forget. The weight she had been struggling under since their last meeting had not seemed the burden it was until it eased. She had felt embarrassed because she was being watched by her family, but it did not remove the light-headedness she had felt at being once more in his company.

She had been selfish enough to be grateful for the promise of another visit. Samson was very dear to her, but nothing in comparison when she thought of another visit off Alexander. Amelia had forced herself to acknowledge that the visit would be the last time she saw him, but her heart kept pushing that thought to one side, focusing on the excitement of being in his company once more.

Watching the lane through the window, she eventually spotted Peter leading the way home and ran to put on her pelisse and bonnet. It would take her mind off the promised visit if she helped with the distribution of holly.

Luckily for Amelia, the snow was too wet and slushy to provide good ammunition for snowballs, so she was spared the pounding that would have been forthcoming in previous years. She took some of the holly from Benjamin and followed the group as they entered the house.

Just as she was brushing her boots on the boot scrapper a movement caught her eye, and her heart lurched when she realised that two figures and a large dog where making their way along the same pathway her brothers had walked only a few moments before.

She held back from entering the house, placing the holly out of the way of the doorway. Samson would be wet and probably smelly; it would be best if her mother did not meet the dog in such a state. Amelia thought it best to work out a way of keeping the two apart.

Amelia walked to the waist-high boundary wall that separated the front garden from the wide-open lane that passed by the house. She stood at the open gateway with a welcoming smile on her face.

Samson pulled more than usual in his hurry to reach Amelia, but Alexander had the dog under control. When they were within a few feet of Amelia, Samson, unable to contain himself any further, lurched at her with an excited yelp, pulling Alexander with him.

Amelia and Richard were to think later that it was as if time had slowed. Samson's jump knocked Amelia from her feet, landing her in the slush of the lane. The force of the pull was so unexpected and with such strength that Alexander did not have time to prepare himself for such an extreme shift in balance. He seemed to follow the dog through the air, but in an effort to prevent landing on where he presumed Samson and Amelia where, he twisted himself away and instead of falling onto the two bodies intertwined on the ground he hit the boundary wall with a sickening thud.

The cry that followed the action would haunt Amelia for months afterwards; Alexander rolled away from the wall, his greatcoat soaking up the slush he was rolling in. The wetness was ignored while he grabbed hold of his head, rolling around in pain. Amelia could see the blood running through Alexander's fingers and struggled to push Samson off her in an effort to reach Alexander.

Richard reached his friend first and pulled his handkerchief out of his pocket and bent to Alexander, pushing the material onto the wound. Richard gritted his teeth; the wound was bleeding profusely. "Alex?" he said urgently, amazed that his friend was not already in an unconscious heap on the ground.

"Richard? Oh, good God Richard!" Alexander groaned, his face a sickening green colour.

"Alex, we need to get you inside."

"No! Richard. Get. Doctor. Johnson," Alexander said through gritted teeth.

"Yes, later. We need to get you inside first," Richard insisted.

"No! Richard, I need him here now!" Alexander said. "Richard, I need him! Now!"

Amelia had moved to Alexander's side. The other members of Amelia's family had moved outside at the noise but were holding back slightly. "Mr Critchley, please go and send a message to Dr Johnson. Captain Worthington needs to be seen by him urgently. We will take care of the rest." Amelia's voice was much steadier than she felt.

"But—," Richard started.

"Now, Mr Critchley," Amelia said firmly. Her tone was enough for Richard to spring into action, looking to Amelia's brother Peter, who took the concerned friend around to the stables. The luxury of walking was no longer an option, no matter what the weather. Increasing one's speed by horseback was necessary.

"Thank you," Alexander moaned quietly.

"Captain Worthington, my brothers are going to carry you inside," Amelia said gently, while at the same time replacing the already blood-soaked handkerchief with a clean one of her own. She had enough experience with so many brothers to know that a head wound bled more than a wound on other parts of the body, but she was still very concerned. Her heart was pounding so hard she was sure her ribs would be bruised later. Thoughts were running through her head, but she had to focus, so the words 'keep calm, keep calm' were being repeated time and again.

"Miss Basingstoke, I apologise, but I am going to embarrass myself further," Alexander croaked out, before turning his face into the ground and vomiting.

Amelia did not move away; she stroked Alexander's hair, keeping back the thick strands that had come loose from the neat queue he usually wore as he emptied the contents of his stomach onto the slush. When it was obvious there was no more, Amelia stood and allowed her brothers to lift Alexander and carry him into the house. He was taken to a spare bedroom, Amelia following like a worried mother hen.

Peter had returned to the group when he had seen Richard away and now looked at his sister with a slight smile. "Give us a few minutes, sweeting. We need to get these clothes off him. We don't want to be dealing with a chill as well as his injury. You could take the dog out of the room at the same time."

Samson had been at Alexander's side since the fall. His tail had almost disappeared between his legs, and he acted very sheepishly; it was as if he knew he had inadvertently caused the accident.

"Of course," Amelia said, bending down to look at Samson, who had crawled under the bed. "Come on, boy, let's go," she said gently. Samson refused to move, not even looking at Amelia. "Come on, Samson!" Amelia pleaded. Samson whined slightly, finally looking at Amelia, his eyes seeming to beseech her. "Peter, Samson will not leave him without a fuss; I think it's wisest to leave him where he is; he won't get in the way; I'm sure of it," Amelia said with conviction. She could not separate a remorseful Samson from his master. She closed the door behind her, leaving her brothers to attend Alexander.

Mr Basingstoke approached Amelia, stopping her from pacing backwards and forwards across the landing. Amelia had changed out of her wet clothing in record time, not wanting to be far from Alexander, but as yet the door had not reopened.

"I've settled your mother in the drawing room," Mr Basingstoke said quietly.

Amelia was fully aware that her mother was no use in a crisis. How her parent had survived bringing up eight rowdy boys she had no idea and could only put it down to the naturally calm nature of her father.

"How is he?"

"I don't know," Amelia responded worriedly. "His wound still bleeds. I'm concerned that it is his head, with the wounds already there—"

"I understand, but we must let the doctor assess him. Who is this Dr Johnson?" Mr Basingstoke asked.

"I have no idea. I'm presuming he is the Captain's own doctor, but that would lead to delays. He must live in London. Should we send for Doctor Dickinson?"

"If he is still conscious we shall speak to him in a few moments and let him decide, but if he deteriorates I will not hesitate in calling in our own doctor," Mr Basingstoke reassured his daughter.

Eventually the door opened, and Benjamin allowed Amelia and her father into the bedroom. It was a small room, used only to house guests on the few occasions that all the family were at home. With four men and one worried young woman huddled within its confines, it seemed tiny.

Amelia immediately approached the bed. Noticing that as well as being relieved of his clothing and dressed in a clean, dry nightshirt, another clean cloth had been placed on Alexander's wound and was being held in place by Thomas. Alexander was grey, the colour seeming to be heightened by the whiteness of the nightshirt. No heart-racing thoughts of seeing Alexander in a state of undress entered Amelia's head; this was not the time for day-dreams.

"The bleeding is easing, but the move and changing his attire has taken it out of him," Thomas said quietly.

"Papa?" Amelia asked.

"Yes, my dear, we shall send for the doctor."

Alexander moaned a 'no'. Amelia approached him. "Captain Worthington, you are not well; we need to get a doctor to you."

"Doctor Johnson," Alexander whispered, but the words cost him dearly, his pallor going even paler than it had been.

"My boy, your doctor is on his way, but we can't risk a fever developing," Mr Basingstoke said, placing a hand on Alexander's arm to reassure him.

"No, please no," Alexander whispered.

"As you wish," Mr Basingstoke said with a sigh. It was obvious that every word was costing Alexander a great deal, so he must feel strongly about being seen by his own doctor. Mr Basingstoke capitulated for the moment; he did not wish for the guest to upset himself further.

"Papa?" Amelia asked, her eyes saying everything her words could not.

"We cannot force him," Mr Basingstoke said. "I just hope this doctor of his arrives quickly."

Everyone eventually left the room at Amelia's insistence. She was more than capable of tending to Alexander, and she did not wish for an audience while she did it. She had sat with her younger brothers during their childhood illnesses so there was no real surprise that she would volunteer as nurse. Only Mr Basingstoke knew the reason that Amelia could not leave the Captain to a member of staff, and it was not the moment to separate his daughter from the man who had captured her heart. The room quieted, and Amelia sat beside the bed. The bleeding had stopped, but she regularly checked Alexander's temperature. She was not sure if he lost consciousness or not, but he lay very still as if afraid to move and never opened his eyes.

The bedchamber door opened slowly, and Richard peeked in. "Your father said I could see Alex," he explained in a whisper. He stepped into the room, looking like a man who had dashed across country on horseback in diabolical weather; his breeches were splattered with mud and stained with the effects of slushy water. His boots would be handed over to a horrified valet; their usual shine long gone.

"Come in," Amelia said quietly, wondering what state his greatcoat must be in and whether his clothes would ever be clean again. Luckily, the greatcoat had protected his frock coat and cravat. Amelia moved from the chair where she had been seated to allow Richard access to his friend.

"How is he?"

"I don't really know. He wouldn't let us send for our own doctor, but there's been no further communication."

"Stubborn mule," Richard said shaking his head.

"Doctor Johnson?" Alexander asked his eyelids flickering before a wince of pain caused them to close once more.

"I've sent an express with strict instructions that if he doesn't immediately start out for Charmouth, he is to be kidnapped. Is that acceptable?" Richard asked, his usual mocking tone subdued.

Alexander smiled slightly, but he winced at the movement. "Thank you," he whispered.

"Who is Doctor Johnson?" Amelia asked, seating herself on a chair on the opposite side of the bed from where she had previously been seated. It was not as close to Alexander as she wanted to be, but she accepted that his friend had the right to be closest.

"He's the man who treated Alex on his return to England after his injury. He is a specialist with regards to dealing with eyes, although what he can do here goodness knows; it's clearly a head wound," Richard said, looking at yet another bloody scar on his friend's forehead.

"It's so near the other wounds," Amelia responded.

"This is so like you, Alex, a damned—please excuse my language, Miss Basingstoke—pain in the rear. Why we couldn't just have had

Christmas in London goodness only knows! Oh no, we had to trek half way across country with a mad dog!" Richard said, worry making him unfairly exasperated.

"Shut up," Alexander croaked.

Richard sighed, running a hand through his hair. It was as dishevelled as the rest of him. "If you'll excuse me, Miss Basingstoke, I shall leave now. I would like to remove our belongings from the Admiral's House. I need to be closer to my friend."

"My parents will gladly make room for you," Amelia offered, but actually wondered where they would fit Richard in their soon-to-be-overcrowded house.

As if Richard had read her mind, he spoke quickly. "That's very kind, but while Alex seems to be willing to inconvenience just about everyone, I'm not. Is there a suitable inn in Charmouth that would be suitable?"

"The Golden Lion is the best inn and only a mile away," Amelia replied.

"Perfect. If you both will excuse me, I shall remove to the Golden Lion and then return. I think it is wise to allow Peterson to accompany me. He is Alex's valet and has been with him a long time; I think it would be a benefit for him to be here to act as nurse for Alex."

Although she wanted to refute the need for the valet's help, Amelia was realistic enough to know she could not administer to all Alexander's needs so acquiesced to Richard's will.

Amelia was once more left alone and returned to the seat nearest Alexander. She placed her cool hand on his forehead and was reassured he was still a normal temperature. How he had not lost consciousness she could only wonder; she was sure the fall would have killed a lesser man.

If Amelia had been able to read Alexander's thoughts she might not have been so calm. He had never felt as much pain since the injury in the battle of Trafalgar, and that had been a living hell. Sheer will was keeping him conscious; he needed to speak to the doctor and, if he allowed the darkness to envelop him, he was not sure he would come out again. He had focused on Amelia's hands touching him gently; it was almost as if she had not touched him at all, but he concentrated on the feel of her, as if she alone could keep him safe.

When Richard left, Alexander once again felt the blackness try to engulf him. He took slow breaths, trying to ward the darkness away. He sensed Amelia sitting on the chair and with a great effort he reached out to her.

Amelia was surprised at the movement and hesitated. It was when Alexander whispered "Please," that she placed her hand in his.

Alexander squeezed Amelia's fingers gratefully and lay his arm on the bed, keeping hold of her hand. If he could feel her, there was no chance of him losing consciousness. She anchored him, and he clung to the feeling just as he had clung to the need to get his men to safety. That had kept him alive then, and Amelia was keeping him focused now.

They sat in silence for hours but maintained their connection. Amelia still checked Alexander's forehead for any sign of fever, but she never removed her hand from his. A slight knock on the door made her try and pull away, but Alexander gripped her hand slightly, and she relaxed. If he needed the contact, she could not refuse him.

Mr Basingstoke walked into the room and noticed immediately the reason for the flush on Amelia's cheeks. He was wise enough to hold his counsel; a sick room was not the place to start lecturing about etiquette. He approached the bed and looked down at the young man lying there.

"Is there any change?" he asked quietly.

"No, not yet. There's no fever."

"That's a good sign."

"Papa, when do you think his doctor will arrive?" The worry in Amelia's voice clear.

"I have no idea. It depends on too many things to be able to guess. The journey would be easier without snow."

"I hope he rides instead of taking a carriage," Amelia said.

"That would be wisest for speed, but very uncomfortable at this time of year," Mr Basingstoke responded. He was concerned that no doctor would see his unexpected guest for days.

Amelia sat with Alexander all through the night. Peterson had arrived during the evening, but Amelia had sent him to bed, assuring him she would hand over control once Alexander had got through the night. Amelia did not want a fever to take hold when she was not there to immediately send for the doctor; at the moment she was reluctant to allow anyone else to take over her role. Samson remained under the bed not moving or making a sound as if he knew how serious the situation was. Amelia slept fitfully, laying her head on the high-backed chair that was brought in to help make her more comfortable. Throughout the dark hours her hand remained in Alexander's, only withdrawing when it was absolutely necessary. She had the feeling that Alexander had not slept at all, but he was very quiet.

*

If Amelia had realised just how closely Alexander was clinging to consciousness she would have been even more uneasy. He had been told that it was probably pure will that had helped him survive his initial injury, and he was determined he was not going to die now. For the first time in a long time, he had too much to live for.

Amelia was the most important person in his life, and he had nearly lost her. He was not about to slip into unconsciousness and die at this point. He cursed the gods; he was due some good luck for goodness sake! He was terrified of falling asleep and, although he realised lack of sleep would weaken him, he forced himself to stay awake. It should have been easy with the throbbing pain in his head, but it was not.

The night seemed to last forever, but Amelia kept hold of him, her grip only easing when she fell asleep. Over the weeks since he had last been in her company Alexander had often thought of times when he would be able to lie next to her as she slept, but his dreams had not quite predicted the present scene. In those he had been holding her, tracing his fingers along her face and body in an effort to imprint them on his memory. Instead, here he was clinging to her hand as a drowning man clung to a piece of wood.

He wanted to open his eyes, to let her know he was conscious so she would talk to him, but opening his eyes caused so much pain and confusion he was not sure he could cope with it just yet. Dr Johnson would know what to do; that was the mantra Alexander repeated time and again throughout the night and long into the following day.

*

Amelia heard the arrival of Dr Johnson before Alexander realised what it was. It was very late evening of the second day, and Alexander was becoming weaker. He still held her hand, but it was not the firm grip of the day before.

Dr Johnson was led into the room by Mr Basingstoke. Amelia noticed the unkempt look of the Doctor and immediately smiled in appreciation of his efforts. It was obvious he had travelled virtually non-stop since he had received the missive from Richard. He had in fact started out in the middle of the night and had covered one hundred and fifty three miles in less than twenty-four hours. His clothes looked travel weary as did his expression, but he entered the room and started speaking in an authoritative voice as soon as he was through the doorway.

"Now, Captain, what's all this I hear? You've had better days, I believe?"

"I have," Alexander responded quietly, not opening his eyes.

"Mr Basingstoke, Miss Basingstoke, I need to examine my patient. Would you be kind enough to leave us? I promise as soon as I have examined Captain Worthington, I will allow you entry once more. I find it easier on the patient to be able to show what they are really feeling without being brave in front of family and friends."

"Of course," Mr Basingstoke responded. "Amelia, I think now is a good time to take the opportunity to freshen up." His daughter looked almost as crumpled as the doctor did and, although understandable in the circumstances, it was time she washed and changed her clothing.

Amelia stood and reluctantly let go of Alexander's hand. She wanted to kiss his cheek, but she could not be so forward in front of the doctor or her father, so she had to content herself with a squeeze of his hand before she released it. She managed to persuade Samson to follow her. The dog needed to be let outside; he had not moved all night or day. Samson once again surprised her; when she expected him to offer resistance, he followed meekly leaving the room with just one glance back, his tail still between his legs.

When the door closed, leaving Alexander and the Doctor alone, Doctor Johnson opened his bag. He had set it down on the chest of drawers next to the four-poster bed. "Now, Alexander tell me everything that has happened."

"I can see," came the quiet response.

# Chapter 11

"Well, that is news indeed," Doctor Johnson replied calmly. "And why are you not joyous at such a development?"

"I'm terrified to move in case I lose it again. Every time I open my eyes, I'm expecting to be blind once more, but so far that hasn't happened," Alexander admitted.

"Let me have a look at what is going on," Doctor Johnson said. He examined Alexander as much as he was able, examining both his head and his eyes. All the time he was asking Alexander questions. "Describe your sight," the Doctor instructed.

"It's as if I'm looking down a dark tunnel, but only in one eye, my left. The other eye is unchanged. It's almost like looking through a telescope, but the wrong way round. If that makes sense?"

After a thorough examination and more questions, Doctor Johnson sat on the chair Amelia had vacated. "I think the headache will ease with time; it is because things inside have obviously moved. You were very unlucky with your initial injury in that two pieces of metal embedded themselves in your head, putting pressure on both of your optic nerves. As I've said before, if only one had rested where it does, you would have sight in one eye. You were peppered with debris and because of that both your eyes were affected. It appears that the piece of debris on your optical nerve that controls sight on the left has moved slightly because of the blow to your head. The obvious good news is that, by releasing the pressure on the optical nerve, it has given you some sight."

"It sounds as if there is a 'but' in that sentence," Alexander said, still trying to keep his talking to a minimum; his head still pounded, made worse by movement.

"I'm not happy that a piece of metal has been dislodged from its resting place inside your head. There is no guarantee it will stay in its new position."

Alexander let out a long breath. "It could do worse damage than causing me to go blind." It was not a question but a statement of fact. He was intelligent enough to realise what the doctor was telling him.

"Yes, if it reaches the brain, there is no telling what damage it could cause. While walking around you could be at any moment at risk of the splinter affecting something in the brain that would kill you, very likely without warning."

"And yet, it's no life to be permanently lying in bed afraid to move," Alexander said. "Can you operate?"

Doctor Johnson took a moment before he replied. "I could, but it does not come without its own risks. I'd want to perform the procedure in London with a doctor who specialises in this type of operation, but there is no guarantee you would even survive the journey. Operating on the head carries more risks than any other; the chances of dying during the operation are very high, and there could be untold damage even if you survive. The brain is a complex organ to start delving around in."

"You aren't selling this," Alexander said wryly.

"I want you to be aware of all the pitfalls. There are too many for me to hide anything from you. It wouldn't be fair if I weren't completely honest with you," Doctor Johnson replied seriously.

"I could die if I do have the operation and die if I don't," Alexander said grimly.

"I'm afraid so," Doctor Johnson responded. He knew Alexander was a strong man, but operating on the brain was still in its infancy and held many risks, even for the strongest in society.

"I think I need time to think everything over," Alexander finally said. "I'm too tired to be able to think straight."

"Would you like me to give you a draught to help you sleep?"

"No! You know I hate that stuff. As long as I think I'll wake up, I will have no problems in falling asleep. I was afraid I was going to die if my eyes closed in sleep, but it seems it could happen whether I sleep or not."

"Sleep will not harm you at this point; you have done the right thing by staying stationary, but I suggest that, when you are awake, you open your eyes," Doctor Johnson said gently. "Your brain needs to get used to receiving signals from your eye once more."

"It felt as if my head was going to explode," Alexander admitted.

"I can only imagine what the pain and confusion was like, but you must try."

"I will."

"I'll settle into the nearest inn and call on you in the morning," Doctor Johnson said. "I think you need to have made your decision by then; delaying will not help."

"I'll have an answer for you," Alexander promised.

\*

Amelia and Mr Basingstoke had spoken to the doctor, offering him refreshments before he made his way to the inn. They were not told of the conversation that had occurred between doctor and patient, Doctor Johnson sensing that Alexander would be the one to tell others some sight had returned.

Amelia opened the bedchamber door quietly and walked in. Alexander was lying still, but his face had lost some of the strain that had been visible, and it was only a few moments before Amelia realised Alexander was in fact sleeping.

She sat on the seat next to him and watched him as he slept. She unconsciously reached out and touched his hair, gently brushing it away from the new wound. She reasoned that it would not do to have his hair touching the gash, but deep down she knew it was just an excuse; she had longed to touch him since the first time she had seen him. Alexander moved slightly at her touch, which stilled her hand, but he sighed and continued to sleep.

Her heart ached for the strong man reduced to being an invalid. He had been such a delight to watch when he danced: light-footed for one so tall and well-built. He had looked fine in his blue naval uniform, which he was no longer allowed to wear. It was not just the uniform that made him look fine although it added to his appeal certainly; every girl appreciated a man in uniform; but he was as fine a gentleman in frock coat and breeches as he had been in his Captain's garb. Amelia had to put her feelings aside; she had to concentrate on caring for him. If she allowed herself to be overcome by pity for all he had suffered, she would be of use to no one.

Alexander woke just as the watery winter sun was peeping through the curtains. He opened his eyes slowly, almost afraid to see the world after so much darkness. He blinked to try to focus. The sight in his left eye had not altered from the terrifying moment when the fall had occurred, and it had been clear that something severe had happened. He was almost overcome by having vision after so much darkness. It should have felt exhilarating but, due to the pain, it had been a terrifying moment.

He took his time to slowly look around the room, carefully taking in every detail of the small but well-furnished room. He forced himself to give his brain time to process each item it was seeing after over a year of darkness. It was still as if everything were a long distance away, but he surmised that it was because only his central vision was working that caused the strange effect.

The fire was low in the grate, and a small mantle clock ticked away the seconds. A chaise longue was set beside the fireplace. A screen covered the opposite corner. He presumed it provided washing facilities for the resident of the room. The furniture looked slightly worn, but was obviously well cared for.

As his head slowly moved around on his pillow, he was wary of moving too fast. His eyes alighted on the sleeping form of Amelia. She was curled up on the chair next to the bed, her feet tucked up beneath her, her shawl wrapped around her tightly. Her head rested on the wing of the chair with her hands tucked under her chin as if to make herself as comfortable as possible.

It was the first time Alexander had seen the girl who had been in his thoughts for weeks now, and he allowed himself to take his fill of her. Her skin was pale and unblemished; her curls, although unruly now due to sleep and lack of attention, sagged a little at the side of her face, but her hair was a rich chestnut in colour. Her features were pleasing rather than handsome, her nose a little small and her lips not the full rosebud that was so much admired, but he could not take his eyes off her. To him she was beautiful. The face seemed to match her personality completely, and he could not help the smile that formed as he finally was able to see her. Since he had known her given name she had existed as 'his Amelia' in his thoughts. Now he had a picture of his Amelia, and he was not disappointed.

As if Samson sensed there was something different about his master, he crawled out from underneath the bed that had been his home since the accident and stood, putting his two front paws on the bed, raising himself to Alexander's level.

Alexander stroked the dog, admiring the fine specimen that he owned. It was no wonder that Sir Jeremy had been keen to obtain him; he looked strong and capable. Alexander held no ill-feeling towards the dog; what had happened had been an accident not a malicious act, and it meant that Alexander was able to see things he had never expected to since the battle.

Samson whined slightly and, although Alexander quietened him, the sound was enough to wake Amelia. "Captain Worthington! You are awake; I'm sorry! I must have fallen asleep," she stumbled, flushing and stretching out her aching limbs.

Alexander suppressed a smile; she was blushing even though she had no idea he could see her. The flush brightened her colouring, which made Alexander long to be the one to cause all her blushes. Her eyes were deep brown and, even though she had spent two days in a sick room, they shone with intelligence. It was no wonder her aunt had not wished to promote her; from what Alexander could remember of Serena Basingstoke, there was no comparison to Amelia. Serena might be more classically pretty, but Amelia's inner self shone through, and she was very attractive because of it.

He wanted to tell her he was looking at her for the first time, but he held his counsel. He needed to sort other things out first; he was not quite ready to be honest about what had happened. "Don't fret. There was no need for you to stay with me; I've slept all night," he said, still quietly. Although the headache had eased since his long sleep, there was still a painful dull throb.

"I wanted to make sure that when you awoke, there was someone nearby to tend to you."

"Thank you. That is a very kind thought; you always seem to be looking after me."

"It's no trouble," Amelia said, flushing once more.

"You are being very polite; I've been a lot of trouble, and I'm afraid it's going to continue," Alexander said.

"Oh?"

"I need to speak to Doctor Johnson this morning, and then I'll know more fully how things stand."

Mr Basingstoke knocked and entered the bedchamber. "How is the patient this morning?" he asked the pair.

"Slightly more able to have a conversation than I was yesterday, sir," Alexander replied. He watched Mr Basingstoke look at his daughter, and he saw concern in his expression. He had struggled to communicate with others since his accident, but even on such a small interaction he realised just how much being totally blind truly debilitated a person. Mr Basingstoke had sounded cheerful enough, but it was clear from his expression something was troubling him.

"I'm glad to hear it. Amelia, I shall sit with the Captain while you go and refresh yourself," Mr Basingstoke instructed. "Take your time; I'm in no hurry."

Amelia did not look happy at her father's final words, but she left the room without saying anything. It was the first time Alexander had seen her stand, and her deportment was elegant. Her clothing was crumpled, which was only to be expected. The material was a practical cotton rather than the high quality muslins that young ladies with funds to spare wore. The simple, creased dress did not detract from the grace of her movements. Now was not the time to ponder too deeply, but the thought crossed his mind that his acquaintances had let someone special slip through their grasp.

Alexander turned to Mr Basingstoke when the door closed. "I'm expecting Richard and Doctor Johnson but, before they arrive, I need to ask you something."

"I'm all ears," Mr Basingstoke said pleasantly.

"Doctor Johnson explained my options clearly last night; he allowed me the night to decide what I want to do."

"And have you decided?"

"Yes, but one of the courses I have decided on is that, instead of travelling to London for the operation I don't see a way of avoiding, I have it here. Doctor Johnson had doubts as to whether it would be wise to undertake the journey with objects floating around in my head as they are. I'm hoping he'll be able to persuade the additional doctor he needs to travel to Charmouth. My imposition is this: Would you be able to accommodate the procedure taking place here? I know it is a unique request, but I'm confident I will be unlikely to have to battle infections that I would risk staying in an inn on the journey to London, even if I survived the journey."

"I see. Of course, you may stay here for as long as you need. I'm just sorry you are facing this at this time of year," Mr Basingstoke said.

"Thank you. Christmas has not been a good time for me these past few years. Last year I was not in a good place, being angry at everyone for what I'd lost."

"It can't have been easy."

"I think I made it harder on myself," Alexander said sheepishly. "There is one other thing though—" Alexander faltered.

"I'm listening," Mr Basingstoke said gently.

"The chances of—,the risks that I will face—,I may not—," Alexander struggled to say the words, not because he was afraid of what he had to face but because he was realising he would never be with Amelia, and the tightness in his chest at the thought made it difficult to speak.

Putting the stilted speech down to understandable fear, Mr Basingstoke leaned across and patted Alexander's arm. "We will pray that you'll come through the operation and have the opportunity to enjoy future Christmases."

"Thank you, sir. I would appreciate that," Alexander said quietly.

The conversation was interrupted by Richard's arrival. Mr Basingstoke made his excuses, presuming Alexander would wish to speak to his friend. Alexander did not tell Richard the news that he could see; it was as if voicing what he had, he would have it taken away from him.

Richard listened in silence until Alexander had explained fully what he had been told and what he had decided. When Alexander had finished speaking, Richard shook his head. "Alex, it's too much of a risk. Don't have the operation."

"I haven't got a choice, Richard," Alexander explained patiently. "If I don't have the operation, I basically stay in this position for the rest of my life; afraid to move in case the metal moves again and kills me outright. I would rather die trying to fix things than die at an unknown time or day. You know full well that this past year I was living a half-life until I found Samson; my prison walls can't close in even further. It would drive me insane; I've no doubt about that."

"I can see that but, from what you've said, the risks are great for an operation. The doctor would be scrambling about inside your head!"

Alexander smiled. "I wouldn't have described it quite like that but, yes, they are going to be delving into my head. Richard, you know me, I would rather meet death face on, than letting it sneak up on me. I've been through enough to know I can't be like this for the remainder of my days; I would ask you to shoot me now if that were the case."

His eyes flew to the bedchamber door as he heard a gasp at his words. Unbeknownst to him, Amelia had entered the room whilst he was speaking, and it was obvious from her stricken expression that she had heard too much.

"Miss Basingstoke—," Alexander started, not really sure how to make the situation better.

"I had just come in to persuade Samson to come outside with me. I thought he would appreciate a walk," Amelia responded, trying to appear calm. She had no right to feel the way she did; he was not hers, and she had not heard the full conversation. There might have been important information that had been said; she could not judge on one overheard snippet of conversation.

"About what you heard—," Alexander continued.

"It is none of my business; whatever decisions you have to make, you will be supported in them," Amelia said firmly.

"Thank you, I appreciate your words." Alexander wanted to reach out to her; she looked pale and drawn, all sparkle gone from her eyes.

"Samson! Come here boy," Amelia said. Samson followed Amelia out of the bedchamber. He was sensitive enough to know something was wrong with Amelia and responded to her. In some respects Samson was astute enough to know his presence could offer comfort to Amelia.

"I expected at least a fainting fit after what she must have heard," Richard said when he was sure Amelia would not overhear him.

"Like everyone else in our circle, you underestimate her," Alexander said quietly.

Richard looked at his friend closely. "There is something different about you, Alex, and I can't put my finger on it."

Alexander paused before speaking. "Well, I suppose you've never seen me laid up like this."

"No, it's not that," Richard said with a frown. "I can't put my finger on it, but there's something."

Alexander had the perfect opportunity to say what had happened, but he still chose to hold his counsel. Whether it was fear of it disappearing that kept him quiet, or something else, Alexander did not have the strength to ponder. He had more pressing things to sort out first.

"Richard, I need you to do something for me, and I don't want a long discussion about it," Alexander said, changing the subject.

"Go on," Richard said, with a sinking feeling in his heart.

"I need you to write my will, so that I can sign it," Alexander said.

"Have you not already made a will?"

"Yes, but I want to make some changes."

"Alex—,"

"Don't, Richard," Alexander said his tone sharp. He held his hand up to stop any further interruptions from Richard. "I don't want to hear it. She has done more for me than any of my former friends. She helped and asked nothing in return. Who else would do that? If I don't survive, I want at least to know that her future is secured."

"You aren't thinking straight," Richard responded belligerently. He liked Miss Basingstoke, and he could acknowledge what she had done for his friend, but leaving her the fortune that Alexander now had because of his lucrative naval career before Trafalgar was an excessive way of saying thanks.

Alexander felt anger bubbling inside at Richard's words; Richard had no right trying to influence him at this point in his life. "I want your word as my oldest friend, Richard, that you will do as I ask, and if I don't survive, you will carry out my wishes." He noticed the deep frown on Richard's face. "It is my decision and mine alone to make," he said, knowing because of Richard's expression he had to push the point.

"Fine," Richard eventually said.

"Your word?" Alexander persisted. He knew that even if he died, if Richard had given his word, he would not go against the new will.

Richard sighed. "Yes, I give you my word that I will execute your will as you desire, whatever my feelings on the matter."

"Thank you." Alexander then dictated what he wanted Richard to write on paper they obtained from the top drawer in the chest beside the bed. When Alexander had signed the document and Richard and Doctor Johnson signed it on the doctor's arrival, it felt as if a weight had been lifted from Alexander's shoulders. She would be cared for whatever the outcome; that was all that mattered.

Richard remained in the room whilst Doctor Johnson checked Alexander. The doctor had been quick to notice neither friend was mentioning Alexander's sight, so he disguised his questions about Alexander's reduced levels of blindness enough so that Richard did not guess what had happened. He understood that Alexander might not feel ready to tell everyone the latest development.

"So, you wish for the operation to go ahead, and it is to happen here?" Doctor Johnson confirmed.

"Yes. How soon do you think Doctor Clarke will be able to get here?" The sooner the operation was over the better in Alexander's opinion, whatever the outcome. Now that he had made the decision, he did not wish for days to pass where there was too much time to ponder what could happen.

"I took an educated guess at what your decision would be; I haven't doctored you for months without learning some of your character. I sent an express to Doctor Clarke last night after leaving here. I also had second thoughts about trying to move you to London. The risks don't justify the move. I've received a note from Doctor Clarke; he is already on his way."

"Good."

"I'm going to plan the operation for the day after tomorrow," Doctor Johnson continued. "I need this room scrubbed within an inch of its life. I want every surface scrubbed until it shines, and no dogs are allowed in until after the operation and even then not immediately.

The room appears clean, but the cleaner it can be, the less likely you will catch an infection during and after the operation."

"Good luck with telling your hosts their room is not clean enough," Richard said with a smirk.

"Yes, not the most welcome conversation to have with virtual strangers," Alexander acknowledged. "I hope Miss Basingstoke understands it is not a slur on her family."

"There is one other thing I need your agreement on," Doctor Johnson continued. "I know you dislike laudanum, but you are going to have to accept it for at least the first few days after the operation. The pain will be too great to try and brave it out."

"I hate the stuff! I've seen too many good sailors become addicted to it after suffering an injury," Alexander growled.

"Well, you need it in this instance. The likelihood is that you will suffer from headaches for quite some time after the operation. I don't want persistent pain to weaken you."

"I'm not staying on it for months or even weeks! You have my agreement for a few days; that is all."

"As you wish; a few days should help." the doctor acceded.

*

It was decided that Amelia's room would be the place where the operation would take place. That way it could be cleaned thoroughly before anyone entered. Amelia was to sleep on a made-up bed in her mother's bedchamber whilst her room was being used.

Alexander tried to argue against the proposal when he was alone with Amelia during the early evening. "I don't want to cause even more disruption than I'm already doing. You need to keep your bedchamber."

"This is the easiest way for the staff to be able to clean thoroughly. With you living in this room, and people coming to visit, it can never be completely clean," Amelia patiently explained. He would also not see her helping; the Basingstoke's did not have many staff and, to help with their extra load, Amelia and her mother would be assisting with the preparation of the room.

Alexander groaned; he would have to say what he was really worried about. "Miss Basingstoke, I could die during the operation. I would die in your room; that is not the last memory I wish you to have of me."

Amelia flushed, and her eyes filled with tears. She brushed them away, annoyed with her weakness, although it was no real surprise; she was hardly sleeping. No wonder she was acting like a weak and feeble miss. She squared her shoulders; it was time to say what she felt. "If that is what's going to happen then I would rather it happen in my bedchamber. I would be able to feel close to you even if you weren't there," she said quietly.

"Miss Basingstoke—, Amelia—," Alexander started.

The door opened, and William Basingstoke popped his head around. "Are hero-struck visitors allowed?" he asked with a grin.

Alexander had growled at the interruption, but he did not stay angry for long. He turned to the door, noticing the new arrival was very like Amelia with chestnut hair and sparkling brown eyes. Alexander immediately smiled at the impish quality of the boy and regretted that he had not been able to see Amelia when she had teased him in London. Their conversation at the moment was far too serious because of the circumstances. He longed to be able to actually see her at her playful best.

"I could never refuse hero-worship, however misplaced," Alexander said.

Amelia had squealed and run around the bed to envelope William in a hug. "You made it! Oh, how good it is to see you!" She kissed her brother's face until he grimaced.

Alexander was suddenly very jealous of the young man. "How's the Agamemnon?" he asked, trying to be magnanimous about a brother receiving affection after a long absence at sea. The fact that Alexander would have done anything to swap places with William for both instances he pushed aside; to envy the young man was uncharitable.

"In the dock, again, Sir," William replied looking over Amelia's shoulder. "Sister, be still!" he laughed.

"It's been too long, and you never write!" Amelia chastised good-naturedly.

"I write to Mother, occasionally," William said with a grimace.

"Sailors!" Amelia muttered.

"You are outnumbered, Miss Basingstoke; I would be careful with your censure," Alexander responded with a smile. "Mr Basingstoke, I'm pleased to meet you; your sister is very proud of you."

"She hides it well," William responded with a smile at Amelia. "How are you Captain? It seems you continue to suffer the effects of Trafalgar."

"I do, unfortunately," Alexander admitted. "I will curse that French frigate until my dying day!"

"There will be more than you to do that. The navy is worse off without you in its ranks," William said seriously.

"Thank you, but there has always been a surplus of very good commanders. Your sister has high hopes for you!"

William laughed. "She's lovely but deluded."

Amelia pulled a face at William, which Alexander was delighted to be able to observe. It was being able to really watch her that was giving him insights into her personality he would never have glimpsed without sight. He was once again reminded of how disadvantaged he had been and offered a prayer of thanks for the ability to see, even though it might last only a few days.

"Now, I know if you two sailors were left together you would spend the remainder of the day reminiscing, but it is time for us to leave you in peace for a little while. You're beginning to look tired, and I don't want Doctor Johnson taking us to task," Amelia said gently.

"I don't feel tired," Alexander responded. If he was left alone, he would dwell on what might happen; having Amelia near him, he was able to forget everything and just enjoy her company.

"You start to go grey around the edges when everything is getting too much for you. It isn't an attractive look even for a fearless sailor such as yourself," Amelia responded with an arch look. "I shall return soon."

"I thought you were supposed to flatter and indulge me? I'm on my sickbed after all," Alexander said with a feigned sulk.

"Why? Telling the truth has a far better reaction," Amelia said with a grin.

"You haven't got a sister have you, Captain?" William asked.

"No."

"You'll soon learn they have claws to match any cat," came the disparaging reply.

"Please excuse us, Captain Worthington. I need to sharpen my claws on my brother. I will return in a short time, but please try to sleep. You will feel all the better for it."

Amelia and William walked out of the room together in silence until they reached the top of the staircase. Below they could hear the muffled sounds of conversation; the family was never quiet when together, and the added excitement of them all spending a Christmas together had increased the volume of jollity. William took hold of Amelia's hand and squeezed it gently.

"What was that for?" Amelia asked, but she had flushed a little at the action.

"You are sweet on the Captain. I hope he comes through for you," William said, his voice low.

Amelia's eyes once more filled with tears. "He's been told there is a good chance he won't survive the operation. I keep trying to make a bargain with God in that I will never ask for anything else of Him as long as Captain Worthington survives."

William smiled slightly. "I don't think it works that way; at least I hope it doesn't."

"I don't care how it works, I just want him to live!"

"If you'd seen some of the injuries after Trafalgar, you would realise he was lucky to survive. He is strong; that must go some way in his favour."

"I hope so, William. I know my place in society; I know I'm not his equal in any respect, but to face a world where he is not living seems unbearable."

"I don't like to hear you speak in such a way; of course, you are his equal. He's had to rise through the ranks just as we all do," William said with disgust. "But there is no point arguing with you while you have so much on your mind. But believe me, we shall revisit that when this is all over."

# Chapter 12

The conversation with Doctor Clarke was always going to be a difficult one for Alexander. There was a difference between making a decision to take actions that could result in death and actually setting the plan in motion.

"I hope we will soon find the piece of metal that has decided to move," Doctor Clarke said. He was a young man of about thirty. His manner was confident, that of a man sure of his own abilities. "I will need to reopen the scar tissue and gain access to the skull that way. I'm hoping the metal will have created its own opening in the skull that I will be able to use to access it."

"But it must have moved," Alexander said, feeling slightly queasy at the thought of holes in skulls.

"In cases such as this, movement could be of the tiniest fraction. I'm hoping to still be able to see the offending piece."

"And if you don't?"

"I may need to drill a little wider, but not too wide," Doctor Clarke said cheerfully. "We don't wish to dig too much. It's not good to leave holes where there aren't supposed to be any."

"What is the reality about my survival?"

Doctor Clarke became serious. "It depends on how much searching I have to do or where the offending piece has moved to. If it is already embedded in the brain, things will get tricky although I'm hopeful it hasn't because we aren't seeing any symptoms to suggest it has."

"You mean I'm still alive?" Alexander responded gruffly.

"That and you are able to speak, move and function as you did prior to this happening. There are a lot of stages between being alive and dying, Captain Worthington," Doctor Clarke said sympathetically.

"Can I speak to Miss Basingstoke and Mr Critchley before we start?" Alexander asked. He was still in the room that had become his home over the last few days. The doctor had already explained that once he was moved into Amelia's bedchamber, there would be no contact with the outside world for a while.

"Of course. We will prepare for you. Two of Mr Basingstoke's sons will help you through to the other bedchamber whenever you are ready," Doctor Johnson said.

Richard and Amelia both came into the room looking pale and drawn. Alexander held out his hand to Richard, who clasped it to his chest all bravado gone from the easy-going character. "Are you sure about this Alex? It isn't too late to change your mind."

"I don't have any other choice; we both know that," Alexander said patiently. "Richard, if the worst should happen, please explain to my brother and his family. Make them understand that I was not throwing my life away."

"I will." Gone was Richard's easy manner; he was fully aware of the dangers of the coming hours, and if Alexander was lucky enough to survive the operation, the days that followed.

"Remember your promise to me," Alexander said firmly.

"I gave you my word," Richard responded with a quick glance at Amelia.

"Good man. You've been the best of friends, Richard. Now it is time for you to leave me. See you soon my friend," Alexander said, squeezing Richard's hand and then releasing it.

"Take care, Alex," Richard responded, before bowing and leaving the room, closing the door firmly behind him.

Amelia sighed, trying to think of something meaningful to say, but her ready wit and easy nature had deserted her in the panic that this might be the last time she saw him.

"Miss Basingstoke— Amelia, please come closer," Alexander said, reaching out for her. Amelia placed her hand in his and was pulled gently towards the bed. "I wanted the visit to your home to be so much different than it has turned out."

"No one could anticipate what happened," Amelia responded.

"Will you be waiting for me when I come round?"

Amelia's barely checked tears rolled slowly down her cheeks. "Yes," she responded quietly.

"Don't cry," Alexander said softly. "If I don't survive at least I have known you for a little while; I shall always be thankful for that. I have only one thing to ask of you before I get taken through."

Amelia looked in surprise at Alexander; she had hoped to disguise her voice enough so that he would not realise she was crying. Her control obviously was not as good as she had hoped. "What can I do for you?"

"Kiss me. Kiss me like we should have been kissing since your first season, only I was blind even then."

"Arrogant perhaps, not blind," Amelia could not resist saying with a watery smile.

Alexander chuckled. "Come here, you impudent chit." He tugged sharply at Amelia's hand, and she fell onto his chest, gasping in surprise. "Kiss me Amelia," Alexander whispered before touching his lips to hers.

Pulling away never entered Amelia's thoughts. As she felt the lips that she'd dreamed about for nearly three years, she put her hands around Alexander's neck and deepened the kiss. Alexander groaned, pulling Amelia closer, running his hands along her body. The kisses were intense, full of passion, expressing the longing and fear that could not be voiced.

Both had wanted the embrace to happen. Alexander had not been longing for the months, even years, that Amelia had but since he had first spoken to her on that fateful night, he had wanted to touch her, to feel her. He explored her mouth fully, teasing her and pushing aside any hesitation her inexperience caused as she returned his kisses. Alexander brushed his long nose against her small, button-shaped one and nibbled her lips.

"You're beautiful; never forget that," Alexander whispered.

"You don't need to say that," Amelia replied.

"I want to because it is the truth," Alexander insisted. "Never doubt that I appreciate everything about you from the way you make me laugh to the way you hold yourself when you walk."

"But—," Amelia started.

"There's nothing else to add. I think you are the most beautiful person I have ever met, and if I am fortunate enough to get through the coming days I promise to kiss you more. A lot more," Alexander said, ending his words with a kiss that felt as if he had poured every last emotion he had within him into it.

A gentle knock on the door made Amelia spring up from her half-lying, half-standing position on Alexander's chest. She turned from the doorway, knowing it was time for him to leave her.

"Captain, are you ready?" William asked.

"As ready as I'll ever be," Alexander replied; the pounding of his heart had nothing to do with nerves at what was to come. "Wish me luck," he said quietly to Amelia as the door was opened fully, and William and Peter entered.

"Don't leave me," Amelia whispered, knowing her words were heard by her brothers, but it was no longer the time for hesitation.

*

The drawing room was the focus of attention for the next few hours. If Amelia and Richard could have had their way they would have stayed outside the bedchamber door that the two doctor's worked behind. Mr Basingstoke insisted they would only cause distractions and directed them both to the drawing room.

Amelia sat close to Richard. They had not got off on the best of starts because of Amelia's London family, but they were united in wanting the best outcome for Alexander. Occasionally one of them would reach out and squeeze the hand of the other in reassurance.

Mrs Basingstoke retired to her room; she did not like to be distressed and could ignore the sombre mood of the house if she removed herself from it. The brothers that were already home entertained themselves quietly. All had met the Captain and each had their suspicions about his interest in their sister. Samson stayed next to Amelia. Whenever she moved, he moved. Each time she did not lead him to his owner he would settle down with a heartfelt sigh and continue watching the door. It had been a battle to prevent him from entering Amelia's bedchamber when Alexander had been carried in, but for once Samson had been held back.

Amelia spent the time worrying herself sick and replaying the kisses they had shared. She put it down to fear of dying that had caused Alexander to act in such a way, but she could not quite suppress the bubble of happiness that emerged every time she replayed the memory of having her lips ravished by the man of her dreams. She would not presume anything more would happen, even if he did survive his latest ordeal, but she would be eternally thankful the kisses had occurred.

The clock struck six before Doctor Johnson entered the drawing room. Four hours had passed since the door to the improvised operating theatre had been closed on the world. All eyes turned to him, no one speaking until he had. "He has survived the operation," Doctor Johnson said, aiming his words to Amelia and Richard. "He was lucky that the fragment was relatively easy to find."

"Lady luck saves him again," Richard said, but his voice was choked with emotion.

"The next few days will be critical," Doctor Johnson continued. "I will attend him for the next few hours. Doctor Clarke is preparing to leave; there is nothing more he can do; only time and nursing can help him now."

"Can we see him?" Amelia asked. She was shaking slightly, and Richard put his arm around her in support. They had moved beyond the social niceties usually shared by slight acquaintances.

"No, I'm afraid not. I want to try and avoid him getting a fever; he would be too weak to fight it. When he is past the next day or so, maybe. For now, the only people allowed in the room are myself and Peterson, his valet. He will be providing the nursing care."

Mr Basingstoke left the room with the doctor, and the brothers continued with their game, allowing Amelia and Richard a little privacy. "He's alive," Amelia whispered.

"Thank God," Richard said with feeling. Amelia took a few deep breaths. "Miss Basingstoke, are you feeling ill?"

"I feel a little overwrought," Amelia acknowledged, putting her hand on her chest to try and remain in control. She had the overwhelming urge to burst into tears, something she would never normally do. "I need to leave the room before I embarrass myself, Mr Critchley. Please excuse me." Amelia stood and moved to the door. William followed her, indicating to Richard that he should not follow as the young man had seemed inclined to do.

"Come here, sister of mine," William said gently as he reached Amelia who had paused at the bottom of the stairs as if not quite sure of what to do. Normally she would have sought solace in her own bedchamber, but she could not at the moment. William wrapped his arms around her and held her as her body shook while she struggled to maintain control. "He's through the worst of it. Have faith."

"I do! I do!" Amelia wailed, finally unable to hold her sobs back. "I was just so worried he wouldn't make it. He's been through so much; he didn't deserve this!"

"I know, sweeting, but have a hope. He might even be awake by Christmas Day, it's only two days away. Have you thought of a present for him?" William continued to hold Amelia close.

"No, I hadn't let myself think that far in advance. I was too afraid I would tempt fate," Amelia admitted shamefacedly.

"I think you should focus on making him a present. It will give you something to do while the doctor and the gods do the rest," William soothed.

"You must think me a fool."

"No, you are my loving sister. I would expect nothing less."

The pair were disturbed by Richard coming out of the drawing room. "I'm sorry; I didn't mean to disturb you, but I would like to send a letter to Alex's brother. I didn't discuss it with Alex, but I think they have a right to know what has happened, especially while he's getting over the first hurdle."

"Would you like to use the study?" William offered.

"No, thank you. I think I'd like to return to the inn for a little while. I feel suddenly tired, but if anything should change during the night, please let me know; otherwise I shall return first thing in the morning."

"We will let you know if anything changes," Amelia said quietly.

"Thank you."

"I think you would benefit from sleeping in my chamber tonight. Spending the night with mother will not give you the restful evening that you need," William said.

"But—,"

"No arguments please. You look fit to drop. I will stay awake and, if there's any change, you will be the first to know."

"Thank you," Amelia said, before sagging into her brother, who led her gently up the stairs.

*

Alexander had no idea how long he had been asleep, but his head pounded as if cannons were being fired every minute from inside his brain. He had tried to awaken numerous times, but the laudanum was just too powerful, and he had been overcome with sleep time and again.

This time felt different though; he could actually think, something lacking during previous moments of consciousness. His mouth tasted awful and as dry as a desert. He licked his lips to try and generate some saliva, but it made no difference; his tongue felt rough, thick and immovable.

Peterson moved to his master's bed and, with the edge of a cloth, wet Alexander's lips. Allowing him a drink would probably result in sickness as an after effect of the laudanum.

Alexander sighed as the cool water leaked slowly into his mouth. He doubted he had ever tasted anything so welcome. He blinked his eyes open, afraid to do so, but needing to know what the result of the operation was.

The room was dark, but Alexander still had sight in his left eye. The strong, wilful determined man, who had faced the French navy without a hint of hesitation felt his lower lip wobble as his eyes filled with tears of relief. He was alive, and he had some sight! His throat constricted, and he coughed a little, feeling at the same time the tear escaping and rolling down the side of his face. He could do nothing to stop the tear; his arms felt far too heavy to move, but without saying anything, Peterson moved over and brushed the liquid away with his cloth.

"Captain, the doctor will be here soon. He'll be relieved to see you awake, Sir," Peterson said, adding more liquid to the dry lips. Peterson had served Alexander since he was a boy and could only guess what his master was feeling.

"What day?" Alexander croaked, not able to ask the full question.

"It's Christmas morning, Sir."

Alexander relaxed into his pillows, drained of energy once more. He had been asleep for two days, but he was alive; nothing else mattered. He closed his eyes and let the drug overcome him once more, thinking as he drifted into unconsciousness that he hoped Amelia would visit soon.

# Chapter 13

Doctor Johnson had forbidden Amelia and Richard to stay more than a few minutes with Alexander when he eventually realised they were desperate to see the patient, and then he had only allowed the visit to occur during the evening of Christmas Day. The pair entered the room quietly and approached the bed.

Amelia hung back a little; she was wary about Alexander's reaction to her; he was no longer in the grip of feeling his time on earth might be at an end. She was not so naïve to realise that experiencing his kisses could have been an impulse on his part through being in a very trying situation.

Alexander lay with his eyes closed. He knew exactly who had entered the room without looking in their direction; he recognised their familiar footfalls. He turned his head slightly; cannon fire was still going off inside his head, but he could move slightly, and he opened his eyes.

Both Amelia and Richard looked drawn; it had obviously not been an easy two days for either of them. Alexander held out his hand to Amelia and noted her hesitancy when she moved forward.

Before he could say anything Richard exclaimed. "You have sight! I knew there was something different about you before the operation, but I couldn't put my finger on it, but I've just realised— you can see! You reached out knowing exactly where Miss Basingstoke was standing."

"You mean I didn't reach for your hand Richard? Blast it!" Alexander said, his voice croaking, but the humour shone through.

Amelia had automatically placed her hand into Alexander's but, on Richard's words, she had tried to withdraw it in shock. Alexander kept tight hold of her fingers. "You have sight?" Amelia asked, her voice barely a whisper.

Alexander sighed, he did not wish to go into long explanations just yet; he still felt so tired, but he owed them something. "It isn't much sight: central vision in my left eye, but it returned after the fall. I didn't want to mention it to anyone other than Doctor Johnson because I didn't believe it would still be here after the operation. It seems I have been very lucky," he explained quietly.

"But that means, when we—,before the operation—,you could see!" Amelia faltered, her face flushing a deep crimson at the curious look Richard shot her.

"I didn't wish for everyone to get excited only to be disappointed again. Me more than anyone," Alexander explained.

"This changes everything!" Richard exclaimed. "It's a miracle!"

"I suppose it is," Alexander said quietly, watching Amelia carefully. Her expression had changed at Richard's words, becoming more closed. He had no idea what it could mean, but it did not bode well.

Richard smiled down at Alexander. "This is better than anything we could have imagined. Welcome back Alexander!"

"I made you this for Christmas," Amelia said. "It's a little unnecessary now."

"What is it?" Alexander asked.

"I'd embroidered a handkerchief," Amelia said with a flush. "It's nothing really."

"No one has taken the time to make me anything before," Alexander said quietly, reaching with his free hand for the gift.

Amelia placed it into his palm and used the movement to free herself from Alexander's hold. She moved a little away from the bed, trying to not make it obvious that she had moved out of Alexander's reach.

Alexander held the material up to his eyes, trying to see the delicate stitching. Amelia had sewn it so that the picture protruded from the material and could be felt clearly when being traced with one's fingers.

"It's my ship on the sea," Alexander said, quietly. Using both touch and sight for the first time in a long time.

"Yes," Amelia answered.

"It's beautiful, thank you. I will treasure it," Alexander said, kissing the material before tucking it into his nightshirt, so it lay against his skin.

Amelia flushed at the action, and Richard smiled. "You will soon be back to your old self, my friend!"

"I don't know about that," Alexander said quietly, his eyes not moving from Amelia's face. He could sense that things had changed between them, but it did not appear to be progress in the right direction. She had put distance between them, and he did not want that, but now was not the time to speak when Richard was babbling like an excited schoolboy, and Alexander's head was pounding.

"We must leave now," Amelia said quietly. "Doctor Johnson will never let us return if we overtire you."

"How's Samson?" Alexander asked.

"William has taken him for a long walk. We didn't think we would get in here without him forcing his way in," Amelia explained.

"I want to see him soon," Alexander said. "Will you both return as soon as you are allowed?"

"Yes. But we really must leave you now," Amelia insisted.

They closed the bedchamber door before Richard turned to Amelia. "I didn't think I would have such good news to send back to Alex's family!" he said, rubbing his hands in glee. "It won't be long before the great Captain Worthington is back in the fold, and we can once again enjoy all that Society has to offer. Please excuse me to your family, Miss Basingstoke. I need to send an express to Lord Newton; it really is a Christmas miracle!"

Amelia had not needed to speak; Richard was so full of excitement at thoughts of what was to come her silence went unnoticed. Richard had bounded down the stairs and, within a few minutes, had left the house; Amelia leaned on the wooden panelling that lined the landing area.

He was no longer blind. She sighed; she was so very happy for him, but she realised, just as Richard had, how much things would change. Alexander was whole again, or as nearly as the *ton* required him to be. His friends would reappear, and the entertainments would begin again.

Amelia shook herself; how could she be so heartless, wishing that he had not regained his sight? She was ashamed of her feelings and cursed the fact that she was no better than those who had abandoned him in the first place. They wanted him only when he was perfect, and it was as if she wanted him only when he was not.

Pushing herself off the panelling, Amelia sighed. She was lying to herself; she wanted him whether he was blind, with sight or had only one leg. He would always be perfect in her eyes, but when he was perfect he would never consider someone as lowly as she. Walking down the stairs, she met William bringing in a panting Samson.

"This boy can run!" William said good-naturedly.

"Yes, he's hard to tire."

"What is it, Amelia?" William asked, immediately picking up on his sister's forced brightness.

"Captain Worthington has regained some of his sight," Amelia explained, trying to look as pleased as she should.

"And that isn't something to celebrate because—?"

"It is! It really is, but Mr Critchley has gone to let Captain Worthington's family know the good news and is probably at this moment planning their removal to London."

"Ah, I see. And what is the Captain's view in all of this?"

"I'm sure he will wish to return as soon as Mr Critchley arranges it."

"I wouldn't be so quick to assume that. I know what I saw in his expressions when he looked at you; don't be so quick to presume the worst."

"He did like me; I know that," Amelia admitted. "But it was only when there was no one else. Then I was the best of the bunch; I'm expecting that things will soon return to the way they were that first season, Captain Worthington not even looking towards the wallflower benches, let alone approaching them."

"If he does that, he isn't worth crying over, but I can't believe that of him," William defended his hero.

"It was who he was before Trafalgar," Amelia argued.

"A lot has happened since then," William insisted, leading his sister into the drawing room.

*

For days Alexander had not seen Amelia. He was aware she had asked Doctor Johnson and Peterson of his progress every time she had seen either of them, but she had not returned to the bedchamber.

Alexander was as frustrated as hell. Richard had visited and was constantly talking of what they would do once he was well enough to travel to London. It made Alexander's head hurt sometimes and, on more than one occasion, he had feigned sleep to encourage Richard to leave him alone.

He had also received a letter from Anthony. It had started with a telling off for not letting him know the moment the accident had happened, but then had gone on to insist that he recuperate at the family home for a few months. Even Anthony had mentioned his return to the social scene of London, and Alexander knew his brother hated the place! It seemed everyone around him wanted him to return to his former life, and he was feeling overwhelmed.

This was not how things were supposed to have turned out once he had made the decision to visit Amelia. He had not come with firmly fixed ideas, but deep down he had known what he wanted to happen, only now that ideal seemed so very far away.

*

A week after the operation, Mr Basingstoke had come to visit Alexander. Finally, Alexander hoped he would be able to speak to someone sensible.

"You are certainly looking well," Mr Basingstoke said, taking the seat next to the bed. "You have colour in your cheeks, which was sadly absent when I looked in just after the operation had taken place."

"Yes, I'm feeling a lot better, thank you. I want to be able to leave this room, but Doctor Johnson is being a stickler," Alexander ground out, hating feeling helpless once more.

"He is being cautious. It's the time of year that illnesses seem more abundant."

"I know. I've almost forgotten what a normal Christmas at home is like," Alexander admitted. "I'll always be in your debt for allowing me to disrupt yours."

"Having eight young men descending is a disruption; you were not. In fact, it has almost seemed like a Christmas miracle occurred: you regaining some of your sight. I know your friend is calling it one."

"To be fair, it had happened before Christmas Day," Alexander admitted.

"It's near enough to give us the chance to exclaim in wonder!" Mr Basingstoke said with a good-natured smile.

Alexander was reminded of Amelia's no-nonsense, easy approach to life and knew where she got her character from. "Who should I be to interfere with the magic of Christmas?"

"Precisely! Mrs Basingstoke will eat out on the story she has concocted around your miracle whereas I tend to err on the side of being easier to please. Seeing all my children in one place is nothing short of a miracle to me."

"You are very lucky with the size and closeness of your family," Alexander said.

"I am indeed, but you have your own family and a very good friend as well. Mr Critchley has been quite excited about the antics the two of you will be embarking on in the New Year."

"I doubt I will have a free night for a year, if I let Richard have his way," Alexander said grimly. He decided now was the time to ask what he had wanted to since he had first met Amelia's father. "Mr Basingstoke, I have yet another request of you."

"Oh, yes?" Mr Basingstoke responded.

"Would you allow me—, do I presume too much when I ask—, I'd be delighted if—, Oh, blast it! Why I'm so tongue-tied, I'll never know!" Alexander took a deep breath."Mr Basingstoke, I would be eternally grateful if you would give your permission for me to pay my addresses to your daughter. Do I have your blessing to ask your daughter to marry me?" Alexander said, finally saying in a rush the words he wanted to say. He flushed, embarrassed at his fumbling and the fact that he had not been able to speak to Amelia before approaching her father.

"You want to marry Amelia?" Mr Basingstoke asked slowly.

"Yes. More than I've ever wanted to do anything before," Alexander assured him.

"I see. I'm sorry, Captain Worthington; I know you have been through a lot more than any young man should have to endure. I cannot let that influence me though; I would not be a good father if I agreed to your proposal. I'm afraid I do not give you permission to pay your respects to Amelia."

Chapter 14

Alexander felt a tightness across his chest so intense he unconsciously rubbed his hand along his nightshirt, trying to ease the internal pressure. "N-no?" he stammered.

"I'm afraid so," Mr Basingstoke said quietly.

"Could I ask why not, Sir? I have a fortune that will keep us both in a great deal of comfort for the rest of our days," Alexander had never begged in his life, but he was about to start if it was the only way to secure Amelia. "If you think your daughter doesn't have a preference for me, I think she does."

"That is exactly the reason why I am saying no to a man that any other father would probably be welcoming with open arms."

Alexander's mind was spinning. "You say that Miss Basingstoke *does* have a preference for me, and that is the reason for your refusal? You wish her to marry someone she doesn't like?" The tightness increased at the thought of Amelia marrying someone else. Alexander struggled to swallow; he was suffering so much.

Mr Basingstoke smiled. "Let me explain a little. When my daughter returned from London, I was disappointed that she'd not received the many proposals I hoped she would when I'd waved her off. Oh, I know she has no dowry to speak of, but I'd hoped the men in your society would see her for what a gem she truly is. It seems that partly, thanks to their prejudice and, from what Amelia tells me, in part because of my sister-in-law, Amelia returned home not having enjoyed her time as I'd hoped."

Alexander wanted to close his eyes and shut out the world. In addition to the tightness in his chest, the feeling that he had a lump of lead forming in his stomach was making him feel decidedly queasy.

"When Amelia returned she was quiet and withdrawn. At first I thought it was just due to her missing the high-life London had to offer, but I was soon to realise that it was more to do with heartache at someone she had met. I'm not breaching any confidences when I say that Amelia was pining over you."

"I missed her like I have never missed anyone else," Alexander whispered.

"I'm sure you did. She had been a good friend to you for some weeks it seemed."

"She had," Alexander acknowledged.

"When she first told me about what had happened between the two of you, I thought, this is it, she has found a match, but it soon became apparent that you had only spoken to her because of your circumstances and not because of attraction."

"We had never been introduced," Alexander said defensively.

"That is true. But let me ask you this; Lord Eckersley had a daughter come out the same year as Amelia; did you get yourself introduced to her?" Mr Basingstoke asked, his tone firm, but showing no other emotion.

"Yes," Alexander said, squeezing his eyes shut with a grimace.

"Yes, the gossip columns were full of Captain Worthington, making sure he was one of the first to be introduced to the newest heiress in society."

"I'm sorry."

"It's a sad way to live, in my humble opinion, but I am just a poor man. That being said, I can't let you hurt Amelia. You will return to London and, if I agreed to the marriage, she would be thrust into your society. Would they welcome her as one of their own, or would they look down at her as you did before you went into battle?"

"My family would welcome her," Alexander said quietly.

"I hope they would, and it is to their credit they don't show the same prejudice that others do, but I suppose we would never know whether you wanted her because no one else wanted you. Amelia explained how you had been shunned; she was justifiably angry about it. My daughter is very precious to me, Captain Worthington, and I'm not going to take the risk with her heart. I want her to marry someone who wants her above everyone else, and with you I can't be completely sure."

"Is there any way I can change your mind, Sir?"

"No. I think it would be best if you left not mentioning this conversation to anyone. In time Amelia will forget you, and hopefully she will meet someone who deserves her."

Alexander's shoulders sagged in defeat.

*

Alexander lay on his bed with his eyes closed. Somehow having sight no longer felt so important after the conversation he had just been part of. He was arrogant; he knew that. He had never for a moment expected Mr Basingstoke to say no. Alexander almost laughed; Basingstoke had said no and in what a way!

The conversation replayed over and over again in Alexander's mind. How could he argue against Mr Basingstoke when everything he said was true? He had only spoken to Amelia when everyone else ignored him. He could try and defend his actions, but he would never have sought her out. It was ironic that he lay longing for her company when he was alone. Questioning his own motivation about what his feelings really were, he lay for hours until Doctor Johnson and Richard were in the room together.

"I want to move to the inn you are staying at," Alexander said, aiming his request at Richard.

"It's only been a week. Are you sure you're up to the journey, even such a small one?" Richard asked. He was desperate to return to London but was not going to do it at the expense of his friend.

"It's time we stopped putting out these good people. I wish to be moved tomorrow."

"There is still a risk of catching a fever," Doctor Johnson cautioned. "The bandages are still hiding a wound; I would hate to get so far to have you become ill."

"I won't catch anything; I feel better every hour that passes. I'm moving with or without your help," Alexander said belligerently.

Richard and Doctor Johnson exchanged a look, but there was no real reason to keep Alexander where he was; he did seem to be well on the way to recovery.

The two friends were left on their own once the doctor was satisfied with his checks. Richard sat down near Alexander, helping himself to tea that was kindly provided by their hosts. "So, are we soon to be planning our removal to London?"

"I won't be returning to London," Alexander answered.

"Not immediately, but soon."

"No, Richard. Never."

"Never? Whyever not?"

"I don't care if I never see the damn place again!" Alexander said roughly.

"Things have changed now; you can go back to the balls. You can dance!" Richard said persuasively.

"And be faced by the shallowest in Society while the Miss Basingstoke's of the world are ignored."

"Alex, she is a lovely girl. I admit I didn't think so at first, but she is a real gem, but she's not who you have always chased. She's not the sort of girl the likes of us marry," Richard said condemningly.

"Richard, will you listen to yourself for a moment? Not the sort the likes of us marry? Who the hell do you think we are? We are the type of people who will only speak to someone if we think they are good enough for us; we are the type of people who will ridicule someone sitting on the wallflower benches because we don't think they are worth our notice. Instead, Miss Basingstoke welcomed me without question and helped me in such a way that it changed my life. Perhaps instead of condemning those who perhaps aren't so well off, we should see what they do have to offer."

"I think you are being too hard on yourself," Richard said.

"I'm not being nearly hard enough," Alexander responded bitterly. "Tell me Richard, what effort would it take if, at every ball we ever attended, we asked someone who was sitting out for a dance? To look at some of the young ladies who weren't the richest or the prettiest would it really have spoiled our evening?"

"Well, no, I suppose it wouldn't have spoiled our evening, but it still would have been a tiresome exercise. I'd prefer to dance with a pretty face," Richard admitted with a shrug.

"How many times have I danced with a pretty face only to find out that she is the most tedious of partners? Or the latest heiress to be nothing but a spoilt miss? You never know; spending half an hour in the company of an unknown could have been enjoyable. We've been very arrogant and unfair. We aren't that special, Richard," Alexander said bitterly.

"We are young, attractive, wealthy men, Alex; what more would anyone want?"

Alexander shook his head sadly, "I can't believe you still think that is enough. Has this last twelve months done nothing to show you that being shallow isn't enough? I certainly need something more."

"Are you telling me you are going to offer marriage to Miss Basingstoke? That's it, isn't it? You think you are in love with her. You are feeling in her debt, that's all. You don't have to get leg-shackled to say thank you!" Richard smiled.

"I am in love with her," Alexander said seriously. "I think I was from the first moment she spoke to me in that godforsaken ballroom."

"Don't mix gratitude with love, Alex. It could be a costly mistake."

"Ha! A costly mistake! You have no idea!"

"What are you talking about Alex? There's obviously something going on," Richard said, concerned about his friend.

"This morning I asked Mr Basingstoke's permission to marry his daughter, and he refused. I'm not good enough for his daughter and, even though I know I've changed, he doesn't believe me. The problem I have is that I'd realised from my previous behaviour how shallow I was; I could only agree with him in his view that I'm not worthy of her," Alexander finally admitted.

Richard looked aghast. "He said no?"

"Yes! And I have lain here all day and thought over his words, and I can't disagree with his arguments. She does deserve someone who treasures her no matter what her background or who her family is," Alexander admitted. "I've been a bloody arrogant fool, and it has cost me the one person I care the most about."

*

The Basingstoke house was a hive of activity. The visitors were leaving in a warm carriage Mr Critchley had hired. The journey would be only one mile, but every care would be taken of the patient. The Basingstoke brothers who remained at home had all said their goodbyes and helped to load the carriage. Mrs Basingstoke had supplied warm bricks for the Captain and Mr Critchley and insisted that a letter be sent to assure her when they were settled into the Golden Lion.

Samson was staying close to Alexander, having been allowed into his room in the morning. When Alexander had moved about, even though he was very carefully monitored by Peterson, it was obvious Alexander still needed the help of the dog to move around comfortably.

Amelia had been absent during the hustle and bustle but, when it was clear that it was time to leave, she could stay away from her bedchamber no longer. She was confused and upset about the turn of events but was magnanimous enough to admit it was as she had thought: he had kissed her when he thought he was dying. She could not condemn him for that no matter how her heart was breaking.

She approached the open doorway and was greeted by the thumping of Samson's tail on the floor as he sat next to Alexander, who was seated on a chaise lounge in front of the fire. He was ready for travel, all his clothes cleaned and looking as pristine as usual. His greatcoat was folded at the end on the chaise lounge, ready to be put on. The only difference in appearance was that his hair was not tied neatly into a queue, the bandage on his head made it impossible to wear his hair neat; the unruly locks were in stark contrast to the normally well-dressed captain.

"Miss Basingstoke, I'm so pleased you have come. I didn't relish trying to find you in the house; I'm still not steady on my feet," Alexander said trying to sound light-hearted. He noticed her pale face and drawn expression and had to sit on his hands to prevent himself from rising from the seat and taking her in his arms. He longed to hold her, but it would be unfair to them both; he had been refused permission, and he had to respect Mr Basingstoke's opinion.

"I'm sure it must be very confusing at the moment," Amelia acknowledged.

"I've missed your visits," Alexander blurted out before he could stop himself.

"I thought it for the best," Amelia said with a flush.

"The best for whom?" Alexander said, but then let out a long breath. "I'm sorry, Miss Basingstoke, I'm being selfish as always. Thank you for everything you have done for me. I can never repay your kindness throughout everything we have shared."

He thinks I am kind, Amelia thought bleakly. Not quite the declaration of love she longed for when she allowed her foolish thoughts to surface. "You're very welcome. You helped with the last few weeks in London. We supported each other."

"You are very magnanimous," Alexander said with a smile.

They were interrupted by the arrival of Richard. "Everything is ready for you, Alex."

Alexander stood, putting his great coat on and immediately Samson moved into his usual place. He placed his hand reassuringly on the neck of the dog. In his first venture downstairs he needed Samson's guidance and confidence all the more.

"Will you still need Samson?" Amelia asked.

"I would imagine I will never be able to walk without him anywhere apart from places that are extremely familiar. Although the ability to see even a little is far better than before, I am still struggling with getting around," Alexander explained. "Samson will always be needed."

"Hopefully not when you are able to return to the dancefloor," Richard said with an easy smile. "It won't be too long before you are back in the fold."

Alexander sent a dark look to his friend. It was as if the conversation they had shared had not happened; he seemed intent on disbelieving everything Alexander had told him. He really did not understand how Alexander had changed and, with the expression on Amelia's face, it was clear that Richard was doing damage with what he said.

"I shall bid you goodbye here," Amelia said, knowing she could not watch the carriage leaving the lane. He would be only a mile away, but she would not see him; it would not be appropriate for her to visit him, and she doubted that any of her family would seek out Alexander when they were busy with their own lives. "I hope you continue to make a speedy recovery."

"Thank you, Miss Basingstoke. Good day to you," Alexander said, holding out his hand in expectation of receiving hers. When Amelia placed her hand in his, he raised it to his lips and kissed it, squeezing her fingers gently with his own.

Amelia felt tears spring to her eyes, but she blinked them away. Now was not the time to show weakness; she had known from the start he was too good for her no matter that her father had tried to convince her they were all equal. She smiled at him despite her breaking heart. "Good bye, Captain Worthington."

Richard made his bow, and the two gentlemen left the room. Amelia could hear the good-byes from her father, mother and brothers, but she remained still. She would get herself under control; she would not turn into a feeble miss.

William walked into the room and, seeing his sister standing so stiffly, a frown on her face and tears in her eyes, he went immediately to her and wrapped her in his arms. "I'm sorry, Amelia."

Amelia leaned into her brother's shoulder, his strength welcome. "God must have accepted my bargain. He lived and has gone to rejoin his former life. It's what I asked for; I just wish it didn't hurt quite so much," she whispered.

# Chapter 15

Alexander had not expected the one-mile journey to the inn to take quite so much out of him. He willingly remained in his bed for the following days, most of the time sleeping. Doctor Johnson had stayed in the area; Alexander was paying a handsome sum for the privilege. As long as there was a chance of a relapse, Alexander wanted his own doctor close by. The medical man was not worried about Alexander's recovery; a patient sleeping for most of the day was enabling the body to recover at its own pace.

Five days had passed and Alexander was able to sit in a chair for some of the afternoon without getting overly tired. A large, fabric-covered winged-back chair had been brought into the bedchamber so Alexander could be comfortable. It faced a sofa, both being positioned near the brick fireplace that kept the room warm. Apart from a screen covering the washstand, bed and wardrobe, the room was bare. It was all clean but sparse. Alexander had lived on ships for years, so he did not need much in the way of furniture and trinkets, but he was not comfortable; he was unsettled and discontented.

He was seated on the chair late one morning when the maid knocked and announced that Lord Newton had arrived. Alexander stood with a shout of happy surprise as his brother entered the room, and the brothers embraced.

"Alex, it is good to see you!" Anthony exclaimed.

"And you! I must say, you have gone grey around the temples since I last set eyes on you!" Alexander responded with a chuckle.

Anthony, put his brother at arm's length. "It is through worrying about my tiresome younger brother!" he responded good-naturedly. "I can't tell you what joy I felt when I received Richard's letter telling us that some of your sight had returned."

"If it was half the joy I felt, I certainly can imagine. Although the first few days were terrifying," Alexander admitted. "Come, sit, let me order some drinks."

The two brothers talked and drank a jug of small beer before the news exchange was completed to the satisfaction of both. Anthony settled back on the sofa, a contented smile on his face. "Richard's letters were full of what the two of you were going to do on your return to London; I think he has really missed the hijinks you both seemed to enjoy so much."

A dark cloud crossed Alexander's expression. "I can't make him believe what I'm telling him."

Anthony was curious. "What's that?"

"Richard thinks I'm just going to go back to how things were before Trafalgar. I know I changed after the battle; those who came through it can't have helped but change, whether they were injured or not. You all saw how the blindness affected me, but it was more than the physical. I could not see, but I clearly saw how shallow and fickle Society was; we had this conversation when you joined me in London. I would be as fickle as they if I rejoined Society now that I have some sight; but to be honest it's the last thing I want to do."

Anthony was surprised. This was the Alexander who would party until there literally was nowhere else to go, who needed the highlife to ease his high boredom threshold. He had purchased a house in the centre of London, around the corner from many of the clubs he frequented; he hated the countryside apart from a hunting trip or racing trip. Alexander was everything that the country-loving Anthony was not. Yes, Alexander had said that Society had more or less shunned him after his accident, but Anthony had presumed his brother would wish to continue his life as before now that he had some vision.

"What do you want to do?"

Alexander smiled a bitter smile. "I wanted to marry the woman I had the good fortune to meet and who I chased here. She is the only one I could envisage spending the rest of my life with."

"And what happened that we are not toasting your upcoming nuptials?" Anthony asked.

"Her father refused to give me permission to pay my addresses to her," Alexander said, unconsciously slumping in the chair.

"You'd better tell me more!" Anthony said in surprise. He was fully aware his brother would be seen as a desirable match for any young woman, especially one without dowry and on the shelf as Alexander had mentioned previously about the young woman he admired.

"She has no dowry; she is not even in the middle echelons of polite society, and her aunt and cousins are the type of people one would definitely not willingly associate with," Alexander said honestly.

"She sounds delightful!" Anthony said sarcastically, wondering why his brother would fall for such a woman.

"She is," came the serious response. "I knew she was beautiful even before I was able to see her physically. She didn't pander to me; instead I felt I had to be good enough for her. She did everything she could to help me, but in a way that never allowed me to feel sorry for myself; even if she hadn't introduced me to Samson, she would've liberated me by just being my being in her company."

Anthony saw the way Alexander became animated when he spoke of the young woman who had affected him so much. He was not surprised his brother had chased her to her home; he knew that, if Alexander fell in love, he would do it wholeheartedly, and it appeared that it had finally happened.

"I had presumed that once you followed her here, I would receive notification of your engagement," Anthony said honestly.

"You obviously have the same arrogant tendencies I do," Alexander said with a half-smile. "Her father quite rightly pointed out I was not in the slightest bit interested in his daughter prior to my accident. He didn't believe I truly loved her, just that I considered being with her was better than nothing."

"And is it?" Anthony asked quietly.

"No!" Alexander almost shouted. "I didn't let anyone know when my sight first returned. I was afraid it was a temporary aberration, and my brain was screaming, trying to process all the images it was seeing once again, so I couldn't face the long conversations I would have to undergo if I admitted what had happened. I genuinely thought my head was going to explode."

"It must have been terrifying."

"It was, which in some ways is a ridiculous thing to say: sight being more terrifying than blindness," Alexander said. "But she would leave my side only when forced to do so, so when I opened my eyes after speaking to Doctor Johnson, I could watch her without her knowing." Alexander thought back to the time when he had first looked at Amelia fully. "It was as if I had been able to see her even when I was blind; none of her features came as a surprise; she was the pretty young woman that I had imagined. Oh, she's not classically beautiful; society would not consider her a beauty of the season, but there is something about the way she is that draws me in and makes me long to spend the remainder of my days by her side."

Their conversation was interrupted by another knock on the door. The maid announced that Mr Basingstoke was wishing to visit Captain Worthington. Alexander instructed the girl to show him up. He smiled warmly when William walked into the room.

"Good afternoon, Mr Basingstoke! This is a pleasant surprise!" Alexander said. "Come in. Please send another jug of beer up," he instructed the maid as she made her curtsey and left the room.

"Good afternoon," William responded with his usual easy smile. "I'm leaving tomorrow, returning to Portsmouth, but I couldn't go without seeing how you were faring and wishing you all the very best."

"Let me introduce you to my bother. Anthony, this is Able-seaman Basingstoke of the Agamemnon; this is my brother, the Earl of Newton."

The gentlemen made their bows and were seated. Alexander poured William a cup of small beer and refilled his own and

Anthony's jugs. "So, you are off once more? I'm very jealous of you."

William grinned. "I shall think of that when I'm scrubbing the deck!"

"You will continue to rise through the ranks. We've all had to do our share of the heavy work; I have the calluses to prove it."

"I love it, really," William admitted.

"Yes, it's been a pleasure to hear the sea once more as I did at the start of my visit to Lyme and, when I'm finally able to leave this room, I hope to see it before I leave the area."

"Are you leaving soon?" William asked.

"I'm not sure; it depends on Doctor Johnson. For once I'm doing as I'm bid."

"That's definitely a first!" Anthony laughed.

"Don't you just love brothers?" Alexander asked drily.

"With seven of my own, I completely sympathise."

"How is your sister?" Alexander had not known how to bring Amelia into the conversation, but Anthony had inadvertently given him the perfect opening.

William faltered a little. "She is well, thank you."

Alexander had picked up on William's hesitation. "Is there something amiss, Mr Basingstoke?" He watched William intently. Not having full vision made it easy to miss expressions, so Alexander was learning to watch very carefully when speaking to someone.

"No! She is not ailing I assure you, s-she is just a little quiet at the moment. If I'm being truthful I would've liked to stay at home longer. There is a ball on Twelfth Night at the Assembly Rooms in Lyme. I should have liked to accompany my sister to force her to enjoy herself, but duty calls, and I cannot."

"Are all your other brothers away from home?"

"They've all returned to their own lives. Mother and father will be attending the assembly; it's the highlight of the social calendar around here, but my sister will attend my mother without one of us there to force her into enjoying herself," William replied honestly. He was worried about his sister, but did not wish to say anything that would break any confidences.

"Does your sister not like balls?" Anthony could not resist asking. The conflicting information he was receiving about the elusive Miss Basingstoke really stirred his curiosity. He was still struggling to understand why Alexander felt so strongly about her.

"Oh yes," William said. "She normally loves dancing, but I think this year not so much. I must take my leave, Captain Worthington. I have a very early start tomorrow; I just wanted to wish you a continued speedy recovery," William said, standing.

Alexander and Anthony also stood. "It has been a pleasure meeting you, and I'm grateful for your visit, Mr Basingstoke," Alexander said.

"I couldn't leave without paying my respects," William said. "I still say the navy is a poorer place without you in its ranks."

"Thank you," Alexander said with a bow.

"Captain Worthington, Lord Newton," William bowed.

"Please send my warmest regards to Miss Basingstoke," Alexander said, as William approached the door.

William paused and turned back into the room. He seemed a little nervous and twisted his stove top in his hands. "Captain, I have to ask—"

"What is it? Please speak," Alexander said quietly.

"If she ever knows I've said a word, she will torture me long and hard," William said with feeling.

Alexander smiled, "I promise you my secrecy."

William sighed. "I want to say something, but I could be being presumptuous. Captain, forgive me, but I thought you had feelings for my sister; I wouldn't go as far as to say there was an understanding, but—"

"I have," Alexander replied honestly.

What William had said was completely inappropriate; a lower ranking officer would never dare to question a captain if they were on ship. Punishment would be swift and severe. Even in the present situation, Alexander could write a letter to those he knew, telling them William had acted without proper respect, and his naval career would be ruined, but the concern over his sister made him speak out.

The expression that crossed William's face was part relief, part confusion. "All my brothers treasure our sister; she is very dear to us, but I flatter myself in thinking I'm closer to her than any of the others. I could see she had a partiality towards you and thought you felt something, if not exactly the same."

"My feelings are very strong."

"In that case, I don't understand, Sir," William said with a puzzled look.

"Why I haven't proposed and why we aren't planning a fine wedding?" Alexander asked his tone bleak.

"Well, yes, sir, actually," William admitted.

"I asked your father, and he refused me permission. He is of the opinion that I would be doing Miss Basingstoke a disservice, only marrying her when no one else would have me."

"If that were the case, you would have all eight of us after your blood, Captain. We might not be well connected, but we would not stand for such an insult to our sister," William responded, his face set into a grim expression.

"From what my brother has confessed to me that could not be further from the truth," Anthony chipped in, deciding it was appropriate to defend his brother.

"Thank you for the vote of confidence, Anthony," Alexander said with a smile before turning back to William. "I would never offer that insult to anyone, least of all your sister, I can assure you."

"So if you reassured my father, why are we having this conversation?" William asked still puzzled.

"Because I could not reassure your father," Alexander admitted. He saw William's expression change. "Oh, don't think I'm not being honest with you, I am. I'm completely smitten with your sister, and I've no idea how I'm going to cope with never seeing her again."

"So—?"

"When I heard your father's objections, I saw my suit from his perspective, and I couldn't argue against it," Alexander finally admitted. "If I had a daughter as wonderful as his, I would not welcome my suit either."

"Are you saying that you consider yourself not worthy of Miss Basingstoke?" Anthony asked in disbelief. He could not be considered a lofty member of the *ton*, but Anthony was fully aware of the lineage of their family and the very real fact that many families would consider being connected to the Newton line as a thing to aspire to. To consider himself unworthy of an untitled young lady proved to Anthony how serious his younger sibling was.

"I'm not worthy of her," Alexander said seriously, turning to his brother. "If I live to be a hundred, I still won't be worthy of her. She is forgiving, accepting of people as they are; she is resilient and magnanimous, intelligent and funny. She is and always will be a far better person than I am."

"Mr Basingstoke," Anthony said, turning to William. "I have never heard my brother say anything like this before, and I beseech you to advise us on any way we can persuade your father to change his mind. Alexander is obviously smitten with your sister and will be a complete nightmare to deal with if he isn't united with her. Please have mercy and save the others in his family from this bleak future."

William smiled. He had been daunted by speaking before his idolised captain, but then to add a Lord of the Realm into his audience had turned his stomach, but he was reassured that both men seemed free of the usual condescending attitude of the higher classes. "It will be my pleasure if it will place a smile on my sister's lips. She is not herself."

"What can I do?" Alexander said. "I'm not eloping with her, and that's the only way I can think of getting around this."

"No, that would never do; we'd chase you and make sure we'd catch you," William said. He was being perfectly honest, his tone was good-natured rather than angry. "You need to convince my father that you do want her above anyone else."

"I'm not sure I ever would change his mind," Alexander muttered.

"I'm surprised Amelia has had nothing to say on the subject," William said.

"She doesn't know," Alexander explained. "I didn't have the opportunity to explain my intentions, and then your father asked me not to mention it; I respected his wishes and didn't utter a word to your sister."

"I'm not sure Amelia would be quite so respectful," William said rubbing his chin. "Father can be stubborn when he's made his mind up, though."

"I'm not hopeful of changing his decision; he seemed firm in his refusal," Alexander admitted.

"Is this the man who faced the French Navy?" Anthony asked with a raised eyebrow.

"Ah, shut-up, Anthony!" Alexander said with a glare.

"Mr Basingstoke, you have been very useful today, and I thank you for your visit, but leave the rest to us; we will work out a way to convince your father, and your sister for that matter, that Miss Basingstoke is worth fighting for," Anthony said to William.

"I'm glad I'll be a long way from here, My Lord," William smiled in return. "I'd love to be able to see Amelia made happy, but if she should suspect I had anything to do with it, my life won't be worth living, even if she did marry your brother!"

William left and the two brothers fell silent, both pondering William's words. Finally Anthony broke the silence. "It looks as if I shall be here a few days more than expected. I shall leave you while I secure rooms then we can formulate a plan of some sort."

Anthony stood and walked to the door, but Alexander's voice stopped him. "If we fail Anthony, I don't know how I'll face a future without her. I was forcing myself to accept that she was lost to me; to have renewed hope and then for it to flounder once more—"

"Faith, dear brother, faith," Anthony interrupted, opening the door and walking through.

# Chapter 16

Amelia dressed for the ball but with no feelings of excitement or anticipation. In some respects she felt as she had when residing in London. A ball was just another entertainment to get through. She had considered asking to be excused but had decided against it; her mother would never allow her to miss the event. Everyone in the locality and from the outlying villages attended the Twelfth Night festivity.

At least this year she would have a fine gown to wear. Sir Jeremy had willingly financed a new wardrobe for Amelia on her arrival in London. Lady Basingstoke had insisted that she was not being accompanied by a chit in drab clothing; too late had she realised that Sir Jeremy would buy Amelia a whole new wardrobe of clothes in response. She cursed Amelia often that the young woman owed them the clothes on her back.

The dress was not as fine as the beautiful gowns that the women of the *ton* wore. They chose the silks that were so fine they seemed to float around a body; Amelia's was made of lilac sarsenet. A deeper lilac ribbon was plaited around the edging of the dress. The gathered bodice suited Amelia's figure perfectly, and the colour of the dress complemented her dark colouring. Pearl combs fixed her hair, allowing more natural curling to frame her face. Staring into the looking glass, Amelia admitted her outfit would fit in perfectly along with the others that would be shown off that evening; it was also a colour suitable for a lady accepting her role of spinster. She would leave the whites and ivories to the younger girls who still had hope of a happy union.

Amelia sighed; she would have to shake off this melancholy; it was no use. She had to forget him and return to her usual buoyant self; this maudlin mood did no one any good. What had happened was over now. She had wanted marriage and a large family, but that was not to be her lot in life; she would have to accept it. She did have a lot to be thankful for, and she inwardly chastised herself for not recognising that. A smile twitched the edges of her lips; at least she had been kissed passionately; that was probably more than many of the spinsters that frequented the benches in every ballroom could say. She would never forget the intensity of those kisses.

She met her parents at the bottom of the stairs and donned her thick woollen cloak. Warm bricks had been added to the draughty carriage that had been in the family for more than a generation, and the farm horses were attached to the front of the equipage—no separate horses for work and pleasure for the Basingstoke family.

The carriage deposited its occupants at the bottom of Broad Street in Lyme, not being able to reach the doors of the Assembly Rooms which were located on Cobb Gate. Amelia pulled her cloak closer as she prepared herself to try and avoid the bustle of the sedan chairs depositing their occupants directly at the doors of the building. The noise of shouting as sedan-chair porters cursed each other hurrying the ones already reaching the doors was overwhelming in the confusion that darkness brings. The welcoming light of the Assembly Rooms guided the guests into its open doorway, and all were once more out of the elements and noise; Amelia was happy to join the throng pushing their way through the bustle.

As Amelia walked alongside the sea wall listening to the sound of the sea crashing onto the stone below, she could not help but be reminded of the longing of Alexander to be beside the sea. To her it was something to admire but to be wary of; she had seen the effects of shipwrecks with much driftwood being left on the shore at Charmouth over the years. To him, though, the sea was something comforting that could soothe him and, because of him, she would always look at it differently when gazing on it during daylight.

The ballroom had a row of large windows overlooking the sea, the impact going unnoticed as the light of the candles prevented any view being seen through the windows. Amelia could not think about the man whom it brought to mind as her mother directed her immediately into the card room. Amelia sighed; she could hear the orchestra, but her role this evening would be to make up any shortages in card games that her mother wished to play. A tedious evening lay ahead; she would rather watch the dancers than take part in card games.

For the first half hour, Mrs Basingstoke did not sit down; she was too busy with her hellos to her neighbours and acquaintances to be distracted by cards. When satisfied that everyone had been greeted, she paused, choosing her position for the evening carefully.

Amelia was surprised when they were approached by Richard and another gentleman she did not recognise. She had not expected to see Richard at the ball and cursed herself for the hope that flittered into her mind that Alexander might also have attended before the reality of the situation made her accept the preposterousness of the thought.

"Good evening!" Richard said cheerfully. "My friend here expressed a wish to be introduced to the finest ladies in the room so, of course I've brought him directly to yourselves!"

Both Amelia and her mother smiled at the pair, and Richard performed the introductions. "Mrs Basingstoke, Miss Basingstoke, please allow me to introduce the Earl of Newton to you both."

"My Lord," both ladies said with a curtsey at Anthony's bow.

Amelia knew immediately who she was being introduced to and looked closely at Alexander's brother. He was smaller than his brother, only slightly but, because the difference in stature was in height as well as broadness, he appeared of substantially slighter build than his sibling. They both shared the same jet black hair and now shared a pale skin colouring, although Amelia thought Alexander's swarthy complexion had suited him. Anthony's eyes were a mix of blue and green, not the blue of the sea that Alexander had. Amelia longed to gaze into those eyes. Seeing Anthony was torture to Amelia; he was so like the one her heart longed for and yet not the same.

"Miss Basingstoke, before Mr Critchley has time to secure you, would you do me the honour of dancing the next two with me? We saw you arrive, so I'm hoping you have not had the opportunity to make prior engagements," Anthony said easily.

"I'm not engaged, My Lord, if it is acceptable to you Mama?" Amelia asked turning to her mother.

"Of course," Mrs Basingstoke said eagerly. An earl dancing with her daughter! It would be the talk of the evening as soon as she had informed her friends who the newcomer was.

Anthony led Amelia onto the dance floor as the three violins and violoncello struck up for the next dance. They moved silently for the first few moves, each watching the other closely.

Finally, Amelia broke the silence. "I hope your brother is continuing to improve from his operation?" she asked. It might be an act of transparency that sophisticated women would never consider, but she needed to know how Alexander fared.

"He does, thank you. It has been a relief to his family."

"And his friends," Amelia said quietly, but she knew at the quirk of his eyebrow that Anthony had heard.

"He has been short of visitors these last few days."

"Yes, my father decided it would be best if we didn't visit," Amelia replied honestly. She knew her parent was acting in her best interest, but it had still felt as if she were being punished, knowing that Alexander was so close and yet unable to visit. "Has your family accompanied you on your trip?"

"No, my wife is increasing again and did not wish to travel," Anthony explained.

"Wise at this time of year. We've already had one large snowfall," Amelia said politely.

"I'm hoping my brother will accompany me on my return home," Anthony said, noticing the way Amelia's expression dropped at his words.

"He will need to recuperate for some time, I imagine. It is a pity you do not live closer to the sea; he would sleep better."

"How so?"

"Oh, he once told me that the sounds of the sea rock him into a deep sleep. I can understand why; it is hypnotising," Amelia said with a smile at the memories of their conversations in Green Park. It all seemed so very long ago.

As the dance ended, Anthony offered his hand to Amelia. When she had placed her own in his, he led her to the edge of the dance floor. "Miss Basingstoke, would you forgo the next dance to accompany me to the top of the slipway?"

"The slipway? At night, with not the roughest of seas, but one that is far from calm?" Amelia asked, surprise in her voice.

"I know it is a little strange, but there is someone seated in a sedan chair who couldn't be here, or he would have entered the room. I think you both need a little time alone to talk things through," Anthony responded.

"He's in a sedan chair? In this weather?" Amelia exclaimed. "The foolish man! He'll catch his death of cold!"

Anthony followed Amelia, a smile of amusement playing around his mouth. He was not sure what sort of reception his brother was anticipating when he met with Amelia, but if her words and the disgusted expression on her face were anything to go by, it was going to be one heck of a scolding!

Amelia retrieved her cloak and wrapped it closely around her as she left the Assembly Rooms; there were still enough people around for her to be able to slip out unnoticed. Every part of her knew she should have refused the request on so many levels, but she could not refuse him anything. Especially as he should not even be venturing out so soon after his operation.

There was only one Sedan Chair at the top of the slipway positioned a safe distance from the waves but so the occupant could look out to sea. The blackness of the night prevented visibility for anything but the spume on the waves, but it was a comfort to Alexander to be so close to the water. Amelia marched over to the chair and flung open the door.

"Have you some sort of death wish, Captain Worthington? I'm convinced you must have! You surely have come here without your doctor's knowledge!"

Alexander jumped at the sudden opening of the door and looked in surprise at Amelia. Anthony had guessed correctly, this was not the welcome he had predicted. "No, he doesn't know I'm here," he admitted.

"You surprise me!" Amelia said sarcastically. "And what did you hope to achieve by risking your health to sit outside when I can feel the chill even though I have been dancing for the last half hour?"

"I have more layers on than should ever be put on a single individual, and my feet are uncomfortable from too many hot bricks."

"You should return to your chamber."

"I need to speak to you first," Alexander insisted.

"I shall visit you tomorrow," Amelia said, needing him to return to the safety of his room. If he caught a chill he would surely not have the strength for another fight so soon after his operation.

"You will visit me with one of your parents, and I will not be able to say or do what I need to."

"And what is that?" Amelia asked. Her anger had prevented the usual formation of butterflies in her stomach when Alexander was near, but his words had caused them to take up flight inside her, and the anger immediately started to ebb.

"Miss Basingstoke, I need to tell you everything. Please join me," Alexander said, reaching out his hand to her.

Amelia stepped back slightly. "In a sedan chair? There is not room. It is not appropriate."

"I promise you we'll fit. Please." Alexander said quietly.

Amelia groaned silently. She could not refuse him, but they would probably be caught, and she would be ruined. She sighed; ruined or not, a spinster was a spinster. Her chances of a match would not be affected. Stepping to the chair, she placed her gloved hand into Alexander's and responded to his gentle pull.

Alexander's heart soared the moment Amelia moved towards him. For what had felt like long moments her words had suggested she would refuse him. He had tried to watch her expression, but he was finding it difficult to see her because of the light. His sight was limited at best, and the darkness made things even more difficult.

He helped her step into the sedan chair, holding her steady. They were very cramped, but Alexander shuffled across the seat a little, and there was just enough room for Amelia to sit. He pulled her closer to himself so she would not be pushed uncomfortably against the wood of the chair. There was a curtain, and Alexander pulled it across the side windows. He did not wish to attract attention.

Amelia had lost the power of speech since stepping into such a confined space with Alexander. Her heart was racing, and her mouth had gone dry. Alexander shifted a little so that he faced her and took her chin in his fingers, forcing her to look at him.

"Amelia, I had to see you. I've missed you so very much," Alexander said, using her given name without asking permission first.

"I-I've missed you," Amelia admitted.

"Good. I kissed you once before when I didn't know if I would ever see you again. I needed to feel your lips in case I had no other chance. Since I woke from that operation I've been haunted by those kisses. May I—?"

Amelia swallowed but nodded her head slightly. Alexander smiled. "I'm so very glad you said yes. I've dreamed about your kisses."

He said no more as he gently touched his lips to hers. She whispered a moan as he pulled away from the gentle touch. Alexander smiled, looking into Amelia's eyes. She looked nervous and unsure, but he saw something that gave him the courage to kiss her again; he saw need.

Amelia's lips parted as Alexander returned his lips to hers and deepened his kiss, letting go of her chin and plunging his hands into her hair. Pearl clips clattered on the wooden floor of the sedan, but their kiss did not ease. She wrapped her arms around his shoulders, longing to grab Alexander's hair but, aware of the bandage, she restrained herself.

Alexander took full advantage of having her in his arms. Last time there was the danger of someone walking in on them; this time Anthony was keeping watch on the outside. No one would disturb them, and Alexander was going to take full advantage of being able to explore his Amelia. When he had finished exploring her hair, she was completely dishevelled, and he moved his hand underneath her cloak. Amelia had stilled at the movement, but Alexander deepened his kisses, and she relaxed into him once more.

Every time Amelia responded to him, Alexander was further convinced she was the only woman for him. He gave into the temptation to brush his hand across Amelia's breast and smiled at the moan of pleasure he captured with a kiss. Reluctantly he pulled away from her kisses; as much as he wanted to continue they had only a limited time together.

Slipping his arms around Amelia's tiny waist, Alexander rested his forehead on hers. "We need to talk," he said quietly.

"I hope you don't expect any coherence from me at the moment," Amelia said with a sigh. "You can't kiss me senseless and then expect an intelligent conversation, Captain Worthington. That's just unfair!"

Alexander chuckled, kissing her nose. "First things first: my given name is Alexander; I want to hear it on your lips."

Amelia smiled. "That at least I can do, Alexander."

"I want to hear you say that every day for the rest of my life," Alexander said with feeling.

"What are you saying?" Amelia asked. Her throat felt suddenly dry.

"I need to be honest with you. Will you listen to everything I have to say?" Alexander needed to be open with Amelia for him to get her co-operation, but some of the things he wanted to say would not necessarily be easy for her to hear.

"I will," Amelia said quietly, watching Alexander closely.

This was it, the most important conversation of Alexander's life, and he could not mess things up. "Amelia, you have such a beautiful name," he whispered, tucking a strand of hair behind her ear. He wanted to keep touching her, but he had to be honest with her. "We both know that if I hadn't been injured at Trafalgar, our paths would never have crossed."

Amelia nodded. What he said was true; there was no point ignoring the fact. "I know," she said reasonably.

"I would have remained that stiff-lipped person I was and would have married some chit, and we would have remained in our superior little world," Alexander said with derision.

Amelia stiffened slightly at his side. The thought of him with someone else was even harder to bear when she had shared kisses with him.

"I'm so glad Richard sat me next to you on that bench in November," Alexander continued. "I look back with shame at what I was before then. I can't even blame my upbringing; when you get to know Anthony more you will find he is nothing like I was."

"He's a good dancer," Amelia said with a smile.

"I hate that everyone has danced with you except me! When I fully recover, if all goes to plan, I shall be flouting convention and dancing with you every dance, not the prescribed two or three," Alexander ground out. "Anyway, I've been challenged recently that the reason I want to marry you is because you are the only one who would have me because of my lack of sight and, at first, I couldn't argue against it."

"Oh." Amelia responded weakly in surprise and shock. "You want to marry me?"

"Of course, I want to marry you," Alexander said roughly. "You are the most wonderful, kind, giving, beautiful person I know."

"Oh," Amelia responded, shocked into silence.

"I would have said eloquent, but at the moment I think I need to revisit that compliment," Alexander said with a smile at the shocked expression on Amelia's face.

Alexander's words did the trick, and Amelia glowered at him good-naturedly. She pulled herself together, trying to focus on all of the conversation and not just the part where he said he wanted to marry her. "So your feelings for me have been challenged?" she asked.

"I couldn't argue against it," Alexander continued quickly. "In some way it was an unfair challenge. We accept that we wouldn't have crossed paths, but that doesn't mean that what I feel for you is any less valid. I never really considered marriage until meeting you and then not at the start. I enjoyed your company right from the first time you spoke to me, but I never considered that having you as my wife was having second best. I came down to Lyme because, although I'd made improvements in my life, thanks in the main to you, there was still something missing. Without being in your company every day my achievements no longer seemed important. I wanted to share everything with you; I wanted to be near you all the time."

"So, you grew to like me?"

"I grew to love you; I always liked you," Alexander admitted with a smile that lit up his face. "I came down to Lyme to see you because I was missing you so much. I still hadn't seriously thought about marriage until I visited your home that first time. I realised we would never be as private as we had been on our visits to Green Park, and that's what I wanted more than anything; I wanted to be with you every moment of every day but without others being there all the time. I didn't want to talk about inane topics with you; I wanted to talk about us. I was thankful for having the excuse of bringing Samson the next day because I was going to take the opportunity and speak to your father and ask for your hand in marriage."

"But then the accident happened." Amelia's thoughts were racing; he wanted to marry her! Never in her wildest dreams had she imagined he wanted her just as much as she wanted him. Well, maybe occasionally she had dared to dream it, but she had soon tried to push those thoughts to one side as ridiculous. Now, he was before her declaring that he did indeed wish to marry her! Or at least, he had before he regained some vision. She paused, ready for him to continue.

"Yes, didn't that scupper my plans!" Alexander said wryly. "I will never forget the first time I was able to look at you. You were sleeping and looked pale and fragile, and I cursed myself because I'd caused you to look that way. It was strange though; it was as if I'd seen you before. I pondered why your features were so familiar to me; was it that I'd actually noticed you before Trafalgar? But it would have been too easy for me to have secretly admired you. No, I hadn't noticed you, but I *knew* you, if that makes sense. All I can put it down to is that, because of listening more carefully than I would have done normally, I already knew so much of what makes you so special."

"I'm not beautiful, and you once said I was," Amelia interrupted, realising that he had seen her when he uttered those words.

"But don't you see that you are to me? You are the person who can say something and make me laugh when anyone else would make me grumble. You are the one who could frighten Napoleon with one glare when she is displeased, but who looks at me with the most love and tenderness I have ever seen; it almost takes my breath away," Alexander said gently. "To me you are beautiful, and nothing you say will ever change my mind about that."

"I think you may have damaged your brain during the fall," Amelia responded.

Alexander dragged her to him and roughly kissed her. He held her face between his hands and kissed her with such force it made her breathless with need. Eventually he pulled away slightly, still holding her face between his hands. "Each time you dismiss the fact that you are beautiful that will be the consequence, no matter where we are."

"I think we may be the talk of society before very long," Amelia responded, but her pupils were dilated with the effects of the kisses.

Alexander laughed. "Good! I never expected a boring life with you."

Amelia pulled away a little; she needed to clarify things. "Are you asking me to marry you Alexander?"

"I would, but I can't," Alexander replied honestly.

Amelia bristled. "Why not?"

"I promised your father I would not speak to you about it; I've already asked for his permission, and he's refused." This was the part of the evening that could go wrong in so many ways for Alexander.

"Why did he refuse?" Amelia asked incredulously.

"He said I wasn't good enough for you, and I can't argue against that," Alexander answered.

"Pah! Fiddlesticks!" Amelia responded. "My father has given me lectures on more than one occasion about us all being equal. Why would he say that to you?"

"He wants what's best for his daughter. I can completely understand his sentiments. To be honest I'm still struggling to find a way of convincing him otherwise."

"Alexander, my brain is mush at the moment," Amelia said. "Please let me try to clarify this; if my father gave his approval you would wish to marry me?"

"If you'll have me," Alexander responded, for the first time not sounding as confident as he had so far.

Amelia smiled and reached up to stroke Alexander's face. It was the first time she had touched him apart from when he was kissing her. "Of course, I want to marry you. I think I have since the first day I saw you three years ago."

"And can you forgive my stupidity then?" Alexander said with feeling.

"If you can forgive my self-doubt."

"What are we going to do to persuade your father?"

"Leave my father to me," came the firm response.

Chapter 17

Amelia stepped out of the sedan chair knowing she could not rejoin her mother and father at the ball. The nicely pinned hairstyle was no more. Even without a looking glass she knew she looked as though she had been thoroughly kissed. A smile turned her lips up; oh yes, she had been thoroughly kissed.

She approached Alexander's brother. "My Lord, I would be grateful if you could send a message to my mother and explain that I have had to return home. Would it be asking too much for me to share your carriage on your return with your brother to the Golden Lion? It would be easier than trying to organise my father's carriage."

"Of course. My carriage is just waiting for my signal to return my brother and myself to the inn. I expect Mr Critchley will wish to remain at the ball."

Anthony gave a footman a message, and he moved into the darkness to organise the carriage; then Anthony left Amelia to return to Alexander while he delivered a message to Mrs Basingstoke. He did not try to persuade Amelia to tell him about what had happened with his brother; her sparkling eyes told him all he needed to know at the moment.

Amelia returned to Alexander's arms, slipping her hands behind his head and pulling his face to her. "I think we have a few minutes until the carriage arrives," she said.

"Let's make the most of them then," Alexander said with a growl and kissed her without further delay.

\*

Amelia paced her bedchamber floor. She had to get this right or the result would be the loss of the man she loved or the father she adored; neither option was worth consideration. Her thoughts had been a muddle since her return home.

She smiled. It had been wonderful travelling in Lord Newton's carriage while having her hand held by Alexander. He had sat next to her, his leg touching hers, his hand holding her hand as if he would never let her go. When the carriage had stopped Alexander had kissed her on the lips in plain sight of his brother. Amelia had never blushed as much in her life, but Alexander had just laughed at his brother's embarrassed cough.

Now she had to try and sort out her thoughts in order to convince her father to give them his blessing. She heard the carriage arrive; it was only a little after midnight, her mother not keen on staying out all night. Remaining in her bedchamber until the voices died down ensured that she would not meet her mother on the stairs when she went to speak to her father.

Mr Basingstoke always enjoyed a glass or two of brandy after an evening out. He said it was to help him reflect on the evening's events; the children all suspected it was to escape from the minute by minute recounting of the evening that Mrs Basingstoke enjoyed.

Amelia picked up her woollen shawl and left the warmth of her bedchamber. The house was quiet as she walked down the stairs; already the heat of the building was being replaced by the chilly air of midwinter. She opened the door to the study and was grateful the fire was still burning in the grate.

"Papa, have you got a moment?"

"Of course, my dear, come in," Mr Basingstoke said, moving from behind the desk to one of the chairs near the fire. "We were surprised that you left so early; I hope you aren't ailing. Do you need the doctor?"

"I'm fine, or I will be after we've spoken," Amelia admitted, sitting in the chair opposite her father. He was very dear to her with his ready smile and calm, quiet ways but, for the first time in her life, she was about to go against his wishes if she could not change his mind.

"Should I pour myself a larger brandy?" Mr Basingstoke asked pleasantly.

"Maybe, although it might be me who needs the fortifying," Amelia said honestly.

"Now you have my complete attention!"

"I would like to receive your blessing to marry Captain Worthington," Amelia said, deciding that the direct approach was the best.

"I see," Mr Basingstoke replied, placing his glass on the side table. "And did the captain explain my reasons for not giving my blessing when he initially asked for it?"

"Yes, and before you condemn him, he agrees with you," Amelia defended her beloved.

"And yet he still chose to tell you even though I asked him for his confidence in the matter?"

Mr Basingstoke never lost his temper, but Amelia could see that her father was not pleased. "Papa, what is your objection to him?"

"Truthfully? I think he does not care for you the way you do for him. The way a man should who professes to want to marry you," Mr Basingstoke said seriously. "I realise that if our neighbours knew of my refusal they would question my sanity that such an eligible offer for my daughter should be refused. I don't suppose Captain Worthington has ever been told 'no' in his entire life."

"I accused him of being aloof before his injury, but he was no worse than anyone else in the *ton*. To hear you speak would suggest that you wish to set him up as some sort of an example as if to punish him," Amelia said her tone quiet, but showing surprise.

"I want what is best for you," Mr Basingstoke insisted.

"And if that is to be married to Captain Worthington?"

"You will be selling yourself short, Amelia. I would hate to see you wilt in an unhappy marriage."

Amelia stood and started to pace the small study. She gritted her teeth in frustration before coming to a stop behind the chair she had just vacated. She gripped the chair in her hands. "Papa, I'm three and twenty. I returned to you expecting to end my days as a spinster. Yes, we all expected me to marry when I set-out on my journey to London three years ago, but we were naïve."

"You are a handsome girl; the lack of dowry should not have mattered."

Amelia looked at her father and realised something for the first time: He was a hopeless romantic. She had always known he had married for love but, until now, the reality had not sunk in with her. She sighed before speaking. "Papa, there are hundreds, yes hundreds, of unmarried girls all with dowries and all prettier than I." She held her hand up to stop her father's interruption. "No. I'm not being overly harsh on myself or fishing for compliments. I saw it with my own eyes. There were far prettier girls than I sitting on those wallflower benches, Papa. Younger, prettier, richer girls will find themselves as spinsters at the end of the season and, no, none of us deserve it, but that is the reality. We decide we are going to try our luck in London when in reality the dowry-less ones of us should be trying our luck where the odds are slightly more in our favour."

"That doesn't mean you should accept just anyone, Amelia."

"No, I shouldn't, and I wouldn't, I can assure you," Amelia responded. "Did you not listen to me when I returned? I fell in love with Captain Worthington the moment I first saw him. After seeing him, watching him during that first year there was no one else I could ever be with. I didn't fully realise that until this season when we started to spend time together in Green Park. Until then, it was just love of him as a figure, but once I got to know him, I was completely lost to anyone else, even if there had been anyone else. I love him, Papa, and only him." Tears had sprung into Amelia's eyes as she spoke, the depth of her feelings only just being realised by herself.

"But if things had been different—"

"Yes, I would never have had this opportunity. I will be happy Papa; I believe he has feelings for me. He might not love me quite as much as I love him, sometimes, one loves more than the other; we have both seen such marriages, but it is enough for me."

"Are you sure you know what you are doing Amelia? I would hate to see him turn away from you when he returns to his life in London.

I'm realistic enough to realise you won't be accepted into the highest circles."

"I've never wanted that," Amelia said with a smile. "I realise there will be difficulties, but he is a good man who is flawed, and I love him dearly."

"I only want you to be happy, my dear," Mr Basingstoke said, finally acknowledging that he could not refuse his favourite child his blessing.

"I promise you I will be," Amelia said, moving from behind the chair and crouching at her father's feet, wrapping her arms around his waist. "You will come to love him Papa, I promise."

"I hope he appreciates you; I really do."

"He is aware that he'll have eight angry brothers and one angry father if he doesn't," Amelia said with a smile and a kiss on her father's cheek. "Thank you, Papa."

*

The day Mr Basingstoke walked his only daughter down the aisle was the happiest and saddest day of his life. He was happy he had seen for himself the adoration that shone from Captain Worthington's eyes when he had turned to see his bride walk down the aisle, but he was giving his darling girl away to another and felt a pang of sadness in his chest at the loss.

Amelia had glowed in her ivory satin dress. The pearl clips in her hair were the same ones that had been scattered on the floor of the sedan chair only weeks before. An amber necklace adorned her neck, a present from William who could not join her on her happy day.

The couple clung to each other's hands as they said their vows, looking deeply into the other's eyes, seeming to forget there was anyone else in the church with them, they were so engrossed in their own little world.

The wedding breakfast was eaten at the Basingstoke household; Lord Newton had insisted on paying for the feast as a thank you to the Basingstoke's for the care they had given to his brother during those difficult days after the operation. Amelia had been thankful that her wedding had not been a drain on the family's resources and pleased at the way Anthony had tactfully addressed the subject.

Alexander had tried to reassure his father-in-law of his commitment to his precious daughter, but Mr Basingstoke had to admit early on during the visits before the wedding that Alexander was proving a doting suitor. Amelia had felt a sense of contentment that she had never expected when witnessing her father and her beloved laughing together.

Eventually the wedding breakfast was finished, and Amelia was helped into the Newton carriage in readiness for their journey. They were going immediately to Anthony's home, but Anthony was travelling with Richard to give the newly-weds some privacy. He was more than happy to hear that Alexander was selling his house in Jermyn Street and setting up a home somewhere outside the capital when husband and wife had the time and opportunity to decide which town or village appealed to them the most. In the meantime they were to stay with Anthony and his family.

If Richard felt a pang of remorse at the news that Alexander was selling his London home, he hid it well. He was genuinely happy for his friend and, if he still had a few reservations about Miss Basingstoke, time would prove to him that Alexander had married his equal in every way.

The London gossips might have speculated about the marriage announcement in the Times for a morning, but in the main, Miss Basingstoke was too far beneath their notice, and Captain Worthington was no longer in the centre of their little circle for them to waste much time on the matter. The news had more of an impact in the home of Sir Jeremy Basingstoke. Lady Basingstoke berated Serena for a whole week about letting a rich captain be won by their lowly cousin when Serena should have had him entangled long before Amelia had her grip in him. Serena sent an insincere letter to

Amelia which was dealt with appropriately, along with the letter from Lady Basingstoke suggesting that Amelia might like to invite Serena to stay with the newlyweds; both letters were unceremoniously thrown in the fire by Alexander before Amelia had time to stop him.

And Samson. The loyal dog remained at Captain Worthington's side until the golden-haired protector was too old to provide assistance any longer. He was then given the most comfortable situation in the drawing room of the Worthington home and fussed over by everyone who entered. He eventually died peacefully in his sleep, having been loved more than any animal could expect.

Long before he had become infirm, a partner had been found for Samson and Bella, a very placid St Johns dog had given her beau many litters of little ones. Ben, one of the litter had stood out almost from the time he was born and was trained as Samson had been. He definitely was an off-spring to be proud of as he took to guiding Alexander just as well as his father had before him and, as such, Alexander still had Samson's needed support through Ben.

Every day Alexander awoke, he would gaze at his sleeping wife. They both appreciated that his sight might not last forever, and Alexander wanted to make sure his memory would be full of images of Amelia even if the darkness returned.

When Amelia started to increase, Alexander marvelled that he would be able to see his children, something he had never dared to hope for in those first dark days after Trafalgar. When in later years his sight did dim a little he was able to rely on Ben more, but his five sons and six daughters all grew up happy to support their darling father.

From facing a life full of darkness, Alexander was facing years of light and laughter because of one young lady who had been placed with the wallflowers unwanted by those who thought themselves the best that society offered. He was forever grateful and in love with his wallflower, his darling Amelia.

The End

## About this book

Dear Reader,

I wanted to write a story involving a dog like some of the wonderful guide dogs that I'd come into contact with when I'd worked for the charity Guide Dogs a few years ago. The dogs are amazing as are the people who put their trust in the dogs, not always easy to do. I could not believe that it costs the charity £50,000 for every guide dog, a huge sum and a massive commitment for the charity. It's a scary thought to be told that every hour another person in the UK goes blind. Guide Dogs works to make sure that their freedom isn't lost as well. The figure for the UK population dealing with blindness is two million. It's estimated that amount will be double by 2050.

I chose a St Johns dog because they were a popular hunting dog in the Regency period and they look very similar to the Labrador Retriever that the charity Guide Dogs uses today. I needed a large dog to be the right height that Alexander could rest his hand on. Size is an important factor when matching a dog to its new owner even today.

You may have noticed a slight difference in this story to other Regency romances that you read. Until Alexander gained some sight I didn't give much description about Amelia. I purposely wanted to try and make the reader 'blind' and hopefully Amelia's personality shone through, giving understanding of why Alexander fell in love with her.

When I started the story I thought it would be a leap of faith by anyone reading because guide dogs as we know them today, really only started around the First World War. In reality though dogs guiding people has been occurring since the Middle Ages. I've copied the following information with permission from Guide Dogs:-

### History of the international guide dog movement
The first special relationship between a dog and a blind person is lost in the mists of time, but perhaps the earliest known example is depicted in a first-century AD mural in the buried ruins of Roman Herculaneum. From the Middle Ages, too, a wooden plaque survives showing a dog leading a blind man with a leash.

However, the first systematic attempt to train dogs to aid blind people came around 1780 at 'Les Quinze-Vingts' hospital for the blind in Paris. Shortly afterwards, in 1788, Josef Riesinger, a blind sieve-maker from Vienna, trained a spitz so well that people often doubted that he was blind.

Then, in 1819, Johann Wilhelm Klein, founder of the Institute for the Education of the Blind (Blinden-Erziehungs-Institut) in Vienna, mentioned the concept of the guide dog in his book on educating blind people (LehrbuchzumUnterricht der Blinden). Unfortunately, no records exist of his ideas ever actually having been realised. Nevertheless, a Swiss man, JakobBirrer, wrote in 1847 about his experiences of being guided over a period of five years by a dog he himself had specially trained.

The modern guide dog story, however, begins during the First World War, when thousands of soldiers were returning from the Front blinded, often by poison gas. A German doctor, Dr Gerhard Stalling, had the idea of training dogs en masse to help those affected. While walking with a patient one day through the hospital grounds, he was called away urgently and left his dog with the patient as company. When he returned, he got the distinct impression from the way the dog was behaving that it was looking after the blind patient.

Dr Stalling started to explore ways of training dogs to become reliable guides and in August 1916 opened the world's first guide dog school for the blind in Oldenburg. The school grew and new branches opened in Bonn, Breslau, Dresden, Essen, Freiburg, Hamburg, Magdeburg, Münster and Hannover, turning out up to 600 dogs a year. According to some accounts, these schools provided dogs not only to ex-servicemen, but also to blind people in Britain, France, Spain, Italy, the United States, Canada and the Soviet Union.

Sadly, the venture had to shut down in 1926, but by that time another large guide dog training centre had opened in Potsdam, near Berlin, which was proving to be highly successful. Its work broke new ground in the training of guide dogs and it was capable of accommodating around 100 dogs at a time and providing up to

12 fully-trained guide dogs a month. In its first 18 years, the school trained over 2,500 dogs, with a rejection rate of just 6%.

Around this time, a wealthy American woman, Dorothy Harrison Eustis, was already training dogs for the army, police and customs service in Switzerland. It was Dorothy Eustis's energy and expertise that was to properly launch the guide dog movement internationally. Having heard about the Potsdam centre, Eustis was curious to study its methods, and spent several months there. She came away so impressed that she wrote an article about it for the Saturday Evening Post in America in October 1927.

One man, a blind American called Morris Frank, heard about the article and bought a copy of the magazine. He later said that the five cents it cost him "bought an article that was worth more than a million dollars to me. It changed my life". He wrote to Eustis, telling her that he would very much like to help introduce guide dogs to the United States.

Taking up the challenge, Dorothy Eustis trained a dog, Buddy, and brought Frank over to Switzerland to learn how to work with him. Frank went back to the States with what many believe to be America's first guide dog.

The success of this experience encouraged Eustis to set up guide dog schools of her own at Vevey in Switzerland in 1928 and shortly afterwards in the United States. She called them 'L'Oeil qui Voit', or The Seeing Eye (the name comes from the Old Testament of the Bible – 'the hearing ear and the seeing eye', Proverbs, XX, 12), and they were the first guide dog schools in the modern sense.

In 1930, two British women, Muriel Crooke and Rosamund Bond, heard about The Seeing Eye and contacted Dorothy Eustis, who sent over one of her trainers. In 1931, the first four British guide dogs completed their training and three years later The Guide Dogs for the Blind Association was founded.

Since then, guide dog schools have opened all round the world, and more open their doors every decade. Thousands of people have had their lives transformed by guide dogs and the organisations that provide them. The commitment of the people who work for these organisations is as deep today as it ever was, and the heirs of Dorothy Eustis's legacy continue to work for the increased mobility, dignity and independence of blind and partially-sighted people the world over. The movement goes on.

## About the Author

I have had the good fortune to live a dream. I've always wanted to write, but life got in the way as it so often does until a few years ago. Then a change in circumstance enabled me to do what I loved: sit down to write. Now writing has taken over my life, holidays being based around research, so much so that no matter where we go, my long-suffering husband says 'And what connection to the Regency period has this building/town/garden got?'

I do appreciate it when readers get in touch, especially if they love the characters as much as I do. Those first few weeks after release is a trying time; I desperately want everyone to love my characters that take months and months of work to bring to life.

If you enjoy the books please would you take the time to write a review on Amazon? Reviews are vital for an author who is just starting out, although I admit to bad ones being crushing. Selfishly I want readers to love my stories!

I can be contacted for any comments you may have, via my website

www.audreyharrison.co.uk

or

www.facebook.com/AudreyHarrisonAuthor

Novels by Audrey Harrison

**Regency Romances**
The Four Sisters' Series:
Rosalind – Book 1
Annabelle – Book 2
Grace – Book 3
Eleanor – Book 4

The Inconvenient Trilogy:-
The Inconvenient Ward – Book 1
The Inconvenient Wife – Book 2
The Inconvenient Companion – Book 3

The Complicated Earl
The Unwilling Earl (Novella)

Other Eras
A Very Modern Lord
Years Apart

## About the Proof Reader

Joan Kelley fell in love with words at about 8 months of age and has been using them and correcting them ever since. She's had a 20-year career in U.S. Army public affairs spent mostly writing: speeches for Army generals, safety publications and videos, and has had one awesome book published, *Every Day a New Adventure: Caregivers Look at Alzheimer's Disease*, a really riveting and compelling look at five patients, including her own mother. It is available through Publishamerica.com. She also edits books because she loves correcting other people's use of language. What's to say? She's good at it. She lives in a small town near Atlanta, Georgia, in the American South with one long-haired cat to whom she is allergic and her grandson to whom she is not. If you need her, you may reach her at oh1kelley@gmail.com.

Printed in Great Britain
by Amazon